PRAISE FOR THE INSPECTOR DAVID GRAHAM MYSTERY SERIES

"Bravo! Engrossing!"

"Such an enjoyable read."

"This is a wonderful cozy mystery. Good plot, good sleuthing, good characters, and excellent dialogue."

"What a spectacular read!"

"I'm in love with him and his colleagues."

"A terrific mystery."

"These books certainly have the potential to become a PBS series with the likeable character of Inspector Graham and his fellow officers."

"Delightful writing that keeps moving, never a dull moment."

"I know I have a winner of a book when I toss and turn at night worrying about how the characters are doing."

"Love it and love the author."

"Refreshingly unique and so well written."

"Solid proof that a book can rely on good storytelling and good writing without needing blood or sex."

"This series just gets better and better."

"DI Graham is wonderful and his old school way of doing things, charming."
"Great character development."
"Kept me entertained all day."
"Please write more!"

THE CASE OF THE
SCREAMING BEAUTY

ALSO BY ALISON GOLDEN

The Case of the Screaming Beauty

The Case of the Hidden Flame

The Case of the Fallen Hero

The Case of the Broken Doll

The Case of the Missing Letter

The Case of the Pretty Lady

The Case of the Forsaken Child

The Case of Sampson's Leap

COLLECTIONS

Books 1-4

The Case of the Screaming Beauty

The Case of the Hidden Flame

The Case of the Fallen Hero

The Case of the Broken Doll

Books 5-7

The Case of the Missing Letter

The Case of the Pretty Lady

The Case of the Forsaken Child

THE CASE OF THE
SCREAMING BEAUTY

ALISON GOLDEN

GRACE DAGNALL

Published by Mesa Verde Publishing
P.O. Box 1002
San Carlos, CA 94070

Edited by
Marjorie Kramer

For a limited time, you can get the first books in each of my series - *Chaos in Cambridge, The Case of the Screaming Beauty, Hunted, and Mardi Gras Madness* - plus updates about new releases, promotions, and other Insider exclusives, by signing up for my mailing list at:

https://www.alisongolden.com/graham

NOTE FROM THE AUTHOR

The events in this prequel take place a short while before *The Case of the Hidden Flame*, the next book in the Inspector David Graham series of mysteries. It is set in the beautiful countryside of Southern England.

The Case of the Screaming Beauty is a classic prequel to the other books in the series, all of which are complete mysteries. They can be read and enjoyed in any order. I've made sure not to include any spoilers for those of you who are new to the characters. Any existing fans of Inspector Graham's investigations will still find plenty of fresh action and mystery, as well as a little background detail on some of the major players in the Inspector Graham universe. All in all, there is something for everyone.

I had an absolute blast creating this book – I hope you have a blast reading it.

Alison Golden

CHAPTER ONE

AMELIA SWANSBOURNE STRAIGHTENED up, wincing slightly, and admired the freshly-weeded flower bed with an almost professional pride. It was, she mused, as though she were fighting a continuous, low-level war against insidious intruders whose intentions were not only to take root and flourish, but whose impact on the impeccably arranged beds and rockeries of her garden was as unwelcome as a hurricane. Amelia was ruthless and precise, going about her work with a methodical focus that reminded her of those "gardening monks" she'd once seen in a documentary. Perhaps, she chuckled, moving onto the next flower bed, weeding would be her path to enlightenment.

As she knelt on her cushioned, flower-patterned pad and began the familiar rhythm once more, she let her mind go where it wanted. How many other women in their early sixties, she wondered, were carrying out this basic, time-honored task at this very moment? She pictured those quiet English gardens being lovingly tended on this very temperate Sunday morning, silently wishing her fellow gardeners a peaceful and productive couple of hours. It must have been true, though, that she faced a larger and more demanding test than most. The gardens of the *Lavender Inn* were spread over an impressive and endlessly challenging four and a half acres.

Guests loved walking in the gardens. They had become a major attraction for many of the city folk who retreated from London to this country idyll. Among the visitors were those all-important ones who checked in under false names, and then, after their visit was over, went back to their computers to write online reviews, the power of which could make or break a bed-and-breakfast like the *Lavender*. The gardens appeared often in comments on those review websites, so Amelia knew her work was an investment, however time-consuming it could be. Keeping the gardens in check—not only weeded but watered, constantly improved, pruned, fed, and composted—would have been a full-time job for any experienced gardener, but Amelia handled virtually all of the guesthouse's horticultural needs on her own. She preferred it this way, but it did take its toll. Not least on her aging knees.

The gardens had proved such a draw and the satisfaction of their splendid appearance was so great that Amelia had long ago judged her efforts to be very much worthwhile. Besides, it was a fitting, ongoing tribute to her late Uncle Terry, who had bequeathed Amelia and her husband this remarkable Tudor building and its gardens. The sudden inheritance had come as quite a shock. Cliff, in particular, was worried that he was entirely unready to be the co-host of a popular and high-end B&B. However, Terry had no children and had been as much a father to Amelia as had her own. It made her proud and happy to believe that the place was being run well and that the gardens had become the envy of the village of Chiddlinghurst, and, judging by those reviews, beyond.

A bed of roses formed the easterly flank of the main quadrangle, within which Amelia had spent much of the morning. They were looking particularly lovely; three crimson and scarlet varieties found their natural partners in the lily-white species which bloomed opposite on the western side. By the house itself, an imposing Tudor mansion with all its old, dark, wood beams still intact, there were smaller beds and a rockery on either side of a spacious patio with white, cast-iron lawn furniture. Further over, against the western wing of the inn, was a bed of which Amelia was particularly proud: deep-green ferns and low-light flowering plants, their lush colors providing a quick dose of restful ease among the brighter hues around them. Amelia took a moment to let the greens sink into her mind, soothing and promising in equal measure. She indulged in a deep, nourishing breath and began truly to relax and enjoy her morning in the garden. Which was why the piercing scream that burst from the open window of the room just above the bed of ferns turned Amelia's blood as cold as ice.

Dropping her trowel and shedding her heavy work gloves, Amelia dashed across the immaculate lawn of the quadrangle and up the four stone steps that led to the patio. Peering through the conservatory doors, she could see nothing out of place. She was quickly through and into the dining room and then the lobby. She took the stairs as fast as her ailing knees would allow, and within seconds of hearing the scream, she was knocking at the door of a guest room.

"Mrs. Travis? Can you hear me? Is everything alright?" Amelia panted, her mind already racing ahead to the horrors that might accompany some kind of tragedy at this popular house.

"Mrs. Travis?" she repeated, raising her hand to knock once more.

The door opened and Norah Travis was smiling placidly. "Hello, Amelia. Whatever is the matter?"

"You're alright!" Amelia observed with a great sigh of relief. "Good heavens above, I feared something awful had happened."

"I'm sure I don't know what you mean," Norah assured her. "It's been a pretty quiet Sunday morning, so far."

There was nothing about Norah which might raise any kind of alarm. As usual, there wasn't a blond hair out of place, and her bright blue eyes were gleaming. If anything, Amelia decided, she looked even younger than her twenty-seven years.

"I could have sworn," Amelia told her, gradually regaining her breath, "that I heard a scream from the window there," she pointed, "while I was outside in the garden. Clear as day."

"Oh, I've nothing to scream about, Amelia," Norah replied. "Could it have been someone else? I don't think I heard anything."

Cliff won't let me hear the end of this. He'll say I'm losing my marbles, that I've finally gone loopy. And who's to say he's wrong? "It must have been, my dear. I'm so sorry to have disturbed you."

Amelia bid Norah a good morning and returned downstairs, distracted by the chilling memory of the sound, as well as its mysterious origin. She could have sworn on a stack of Bibles....

CHAPTER TWO

AROUND ELEVEN O'CLOCK, Cliff Swansbourne returned along the gravel path to the front entrance of the *Lavender* in his battered but supremely reliable Land Rover Defender. A Sunday morning ritual as old as their tenure at the inn, Cliff's forays to the farmers' market in nearby Dorking were legend, both for his chipper, sunny banter with the stall-holders, and for the bewildering array of local produce with which he returned. Cliff was not, his wife had often observed, a planner. The dinner menu seemed to compose itself, in his head, during the course of an hour's purposeful striding around the market, and he always managed to return with ingredients for something sumptuous and appealing that would arrive on the dinner table a few hours hence. From the distinctive fragrance wafting from the back of the Landy, Amelia suspected fish.

"Did you know," Cliff began, handing a brimming tote bag of supplies to his wife, "that salmon can fly?"

Amelia gave him a quizzical look. *Which of us, just*

remind me, is going bloody loopy? "You don't say," she replied noncommittally.

"The bloke said this salmon had flown down from a Scottish loch first thing this morning. Freshest fish you've ever seen," he promised. "I got a damn great forest of dill, too. We've still got those cedar planks, haven't we, dear?"

Amelia carted four large bags of groceries into the kitchen and set them down on their sturdy, traditional wooden table. "They're in the pantry somewhere, I think," she said. "Look, this is going to sound a bit silly, but..."

"You?" Cliff mocked. "Silly? Never in a million years..."

"Just hold your tongue for half a second, you impossible man," she said, bringing him to a halt in the middle of the kitchen and hugging him. "Thanks for going shopping. The salmon is going to be wonderful. I know it."

"Certain as Christmas," Cliff replied. "Now, what's going to sound a bit silly?"

Amelia shook off her reservations and put it plainly. "Have you ever, while I've been out..."

"Never," Cliff replied, his back straightening defiantly. "And you can't prove that I have. I was nowhere near the scene of the event." He paused. "Whatever the event was," he added, less certainly. "Not guilty, I'm saying."

"Will you shut up and listen?" Amelia demanded, punching him on the shoulder as she had done many times during moments of frustration over the thirty years they had been married. "Have you ever heard Norah Travis, or any of our other guests, scream?"

Cliff raised an eyebrow.

Classic Cliff. He won't take this seriously until I make him.

"Scream, you say?"

"I did."

"What kind of scream?"

"Does it matter, you daft bugger? A scream, you know, an explosion of sound caused by pain or anxiety or..." She stopped. Cliff would need no encouragement, she felt quite sure.

"Or... nookie?" he said, wiggling a raised eyebrow.

"Calm your ardor, Romeo. It wasn't that kind of scream," Amelia told him.

"Ah," he replied, a little deflated. "Well, no, if I'm honest, I haven't heard such an ejaculation."

"Cliff, for the love of God..."

"Not once, seriously. Why?"

"Well, I was out in the garden, and I could have sworn there was this sudden, piercing scream from Norah's room. You know, over on the west corner."

"I know the one, darling. I work here too if you remember. But why would she be screaming on a Sunday morning? Realized she'd woken up too late for church? Doesn't seem the type."

Amelia shrugged. "Hardly. And that's just the thing. I ran to her room to make sure she was alright..."

"Ran?" Cliff said. The eyebrow returned skyward. "You *ran* somewhere?"

"I mean, yes," Amelia replied, sensitive to these jabs about her age and her increasingly perfidious knees. "I'm no Olympic sprinter or anything, but I got there in record time. And Norah denied having made or heard any such sound."

They sat around the kitchen table, the overflowing bags of produce temporarily forgotten. "Tricky," Cliff observed. "Very mysterious."

"So what do you think?" Amelia asked, stumped.

"I think," he said, taking her hand fondly across the table, "that it's time we called the men in the white coats."

Amelia stood and lambasted him, just as he'd hoped. "Now listen here, you rotten little sod! I'm not the one losing it. I've never claimed, for instance, that salmon can fly! And what about that time you went into town to get the newspaper in your underpants?"

Cliff defended himself. "It was half-past five in the morning, there wasn't a soul to be seen, and I was trying to save time," he explained. "All about efficiency."

"Codswallop."

"Suit yourself," Cliff remarked, standing to begin finding homes for the groceries, "but I'm not the one imagining screams out of thin air."

Amelia shook her head. "I didn't imagine it, Cliff. It's not like I was smelling toast while having a stroke. I'm of sound mind," she said, wagging a finger at his skeptical smirk, "and I know what I heard."

"Darling," Cliff began, "there are a number of things a lady might do, by herself, in the privacy of her room, on a lazy Sunday morning, which might make her scream. And once confronted with the evidence that she had been over-heard," he added, "what makes you so sure that Norah Travis would be comfortable sharing such intimacies with her landlady? She's been here a grand total of two nights. It's not as though you're sisters."

"True," Amelia had to concede. "But, as I say, it wasn't that kind of scream."

"Everyone's different. It's the twenty-first century, my sweet. People get their jollies in all manner of ways. We mustn't judge, especially paying guests, and we mustn't harass people who are simply enjoying some alone time."

Amelia bent over and aggressively shoved a sack of potatoes under the bottom shelf of the pantry. "Impossible man," she said again before wrenching open the door that led to the gardens and stomping away.

CHAPTER THREE

THE SALMON WAS no disappointment. Grilled to perfection and carpeted with flavorful dill, it was preferred to their standard alternative Sunday evening offering of Beef Bourguignon. Vegetarian lasagna also remained untouched in the fridge. Once Cliff and Amelia had cleared away the tables and loaded the dishwasher, they poured themselves their customary glass of dry white wine and sat around the kitchen table once more. These routines gave their lives a pleasing structure, but also provided a vital time to stop, talk, and exchange news of the day. With so much hurrying around and their reservation book pleasingly full, this was a quiet oasis of time which both cherished.

"Did you notice that Norah Travis entirely demolished her salmon?" Cliff said, sipping his wine. "Damn near ate the bones it came on."

"Well done, chef," Amelia said, raising a glass in salute.

"Didn't hear her scream once," Cliff noted.

"Oh, for heaven's sake. I told you what I heard. And you can believe whatever you want."

Cliff chuckled easily and reached over to a side table for their reservations book. "I believe, oh co-proprietor of mine, that the *Lavender Inn* is just about fully booked, from September through the New Year. And," he added, flicking forward a good number of pages, "in decent shape beyond then. I don't know how we've managed it."

"Bloody hard work," Amelia told him. "My knees have paid for that garden with their very lives. And you're doing wonders with the kitchen and all the supplies. Not to mention keeping Doris on the straight and narrow."

Like a good matron on a hospital ward, a good house-keeper was critical to their success. Doris Tisbury was second to none. "She needs no help from me," Cliff demurred. "I'd trust her with everything from a double-booking to a Jihadist insurgency."

"Let's hope it doesn't come to that. I've just got the garden looking splendid," Amelia replied, deadpan.

"You have indeed, my sweet," Cliff said, acknowledging her comment with a salute of his wine glass. "What I'm saying is, you know, with business being so good, we might revisit the idea of, you know..."

"'Sodding off to Mexico'?" Amelia quoted. "Isn't that how you put it? Seriously, that old plan again?"

"It's not old, but it's certainly a plan. And a good one," Cliff said, topping off both their glasses. "Think about it. White sandy beaches," he said, his gestures becoming expansive, "hammocks slung between two palm trees... Tell me you don't daydream about it. Because I most certainly do."

Amelia couldn't resist. "When you're not daydreaming about what might make the delectable Norah Travis scream."

"A man is permitted his fantasies," Cliff replied. "But

I'm serious, darling. We've worked bloody hard, as you so rightly observed, and there's going to be plenty of money coming in, especially once the rates go up for the festive season. I mean, you've seen the bookings..."

"I've seen them, and they're fantastic," Amelia replied, leaving the important and inevitable 'but' unsaid.

"Not now," Cliff concluded. "You've said that before. More than once." His disappointment was real, and he refused to hide it. Forty years of work as a structural engineer, then an assessor, then a trainer and mentor to the young 'uns.... He was ready to put aside ownership of the *Lavender* and get on with his master plan for retirement by lying on warm, dry sand, dipping his toes in the Pacific, and having someone bring him martinis on the hour. But month by month, he could feel it slipping away.

"We need more time, and we need more money," Amelia told him, ever the practical one of the pair. "Even if we sold up tomorrow, how long do you really think the money would last?"

"Depends if you let me blow the whole lot on coke and strippers," Cliff joked.

She took his hand. "Darling," she began, still deadpan, as was their way, "I know it's your life's dream to snort Bolivian marching powder off some pretty girl's unmentionables, but I need you here, with me, on planet Earth. Just for a couple more years."

Cliff was deflated, despite his fooling around. "Well, bugger."

"I'm sorry. Soon, I promise. All the strippers in Tijuana."

Cliff finished his wine and gave his wife a smile laden with subtle meanings. "I love you and I trust you. We're a team, and this is where I belong. Just don't promise paradise and then deliver another four years of fishing the pin-bones out of salmon and chopping up mountains of dill. I couldn't take it."

They finished their wine and Amelia headed to bed. Cliff sat in the kitchen for longer than he would have chosen, picturing the simple, relaxed life he had worked so hard for. *She's right, again. As always. Why did she have to be so damned pragmatic?*

It was Amelia who had steered him away from those expensive and alluring mid-life distractions, twenty years ago: the sports car, not unexpected but certainly expensive; the mad, medically inadvisable plan to hike from Lands' End to John O'Groats *and back again*; and his simmering, exotic pipe-dream of a beach retirement in Mexico.

The arguments had been fierce, but once he understood that she loved him and wanted to help, he realized that he had floated a little adrift as he hit forty-five. They needed a solid plan, not a high-end fancy pair of wheels worth four years of his old salary. It was then that a peaceable calm returned to the Swansbourne household. Amelia had stood by him as he'd shrugged off the "bloody nonsense," as he'd taken to calling it and risen to the top of his profession. She would stand by him now, he felt sure.

Remarkable woman, he reflected as he turned out the lights and headed upstairs. For a second, a noise from outside pierced his consciousness but he shook his head and turned back to his musings. *Wouldn't trade her in. Not for anything. Not even for a luxury yacht full of strippers.*

CHAPTER FOUR

DORIS TISBURY WHEELED her cart, piled high with towels and sheets, along the second-floor hallway of the *Lavender*, humming a tune which had been stuck in her head all morning. Was it Tchaikovsky? Or from an opera? She couldn't remember, but it was a jaunty, upbeat tune that fit her mood. There was cleaning to be done. Each time Doris closed the door on a room she knew now to be immaculate, there was a tiny jolt of satisfaction. The world was as it should be, everything was in its place. Doris made emphatically sure of it.

Approaching sixty and with the sturdy forearms of an artisan baker, Doris was originally a "Yorkshire lass" and currently a no-nonsense housekeeper. She had infinite patience for the tedious chores with which she was tasked but absolutely none whatsoever with people who "mucked about," as she put it. Her children and grandchildren knew this expression far too well. The penalties for "mucking about" were the forfeiture of dessert, or pocket money, or—horror of horrors—additional household chores. Doris was no brute, but rather a disciplinarian. She believed that quality and rigor and getting things done without fuss or delay was what was required for an upstanding life. She brought a forthright thoroughness to the *Lavender*, and the inn thrived, in good measure, due to her firm dedication to duty.

Most of the *Lavender's* guests were early risers. They might wish to travel to one of the attractions close by or in London or enjoy one of Cliff's massive, traditional, cooked breakfasts. Some took in the gardens with an early morning stroll. On the odd occasion this might not be the case, however. Doris would knock, wait a polite interval, enter the room, and find the guest either still asleep, or doing something they'd rather Doris had not seen. She'd have dared to boast that, during her years at the *Lavender* and at other hotels previously, she had been exposed to just about every sordid human pastime, whether it was happening right in front of her, or through the casual discarding of incriminating evidence. Nothing could shock Doris, she would claim. Not even that business last year with the Maltese businessman and his suitcase full of...well, let's not think on that.

Norah Travis' door was next. Doris knocked her accustomed three times, calling through, "Housekeeping!" in as bright a tone as she could manage and knocked again. She counted to five, as she always did—just to lessen the frequency of those awkward encounters—and then used her master key to open the door.

Doris peered into the room. The bed had not been slept in, there was no doubt about it. Even if Norah had, for some reason, chosen to make it herself, there's no way she'd have matched the precise, geometrical perfection that Doris brought to her work. There was certainly no sign of the young lady.

Doris patrolled the room, emptying the trash can and giving the dresser a little squirt of furniture polish. The room smelled slightly musty, so Doris opened both of the windows to air the place out. Then she stepped toward the bathroom, anticipating the usual towels on the floor. Instead, she was shocked to look down and see the soles of a pair of shoes. As Doris pushed the door further open, she saw that the shoes were attached to Norah Travis and that the woman was sprawled on the bathroom floor, immobile.

"Ms. Travis?" Doris breathed. "Oh, goodness, I'll get help, dear..." But as she turned, she saw that Norah's once-pretty face and long blond hair were thickly coated with blood that was staining her blue blouse and that the skin of her exposed neck and shoulders was an unearthly, alabaster white.

CHAPTER FIVE

CLIFF LOOKED UP from tossing a giant bowl of salad as Doris rushed into the kitchen. He knew at once that something terrible had happened.

"It's Norah Travis," Doris managed to say, hands to her mouth, but then the grim news stuck in her throat and wouldn't come out.

"Doris?" Cliff said, dropping the salad tongs and walking across the kitchen to his dumbstruck housekeeper. "Doris, what's happened? Is something wrong?" The awful truth was etched on Doris' face so clearly that Cliff needn't have asked.

"She's dead, Mr. Swansbourne," Doris said, finding her voice at last. "In the bathroom. On the floor."

"Jesus." Cliff was away, taking the stairs two at a time. When he arrived at the door of Norah's en-suite, one glance told him everything. The attractive blond was beyond all help and had been for some hours. A guest of the *Lavender* dead. Cliff gasped, recoiling from the sight, and seized the wooden doorframe for support. "Oh, no." Amelia had gone to the local nursery, one of her favorite places, for seedlings. There was no telling when she would be back. The weight of the responsibility that bore down on Cliff as he stared at Norah's body frightened him.

"Cliff? What's wrong?" Cliff looked up to see a familiar face. It was Tim Lloyd, a guest so regular he was almost a family friend. "Oh, God, is it Norah?" Tim asked, brazenly stepping past Cliff into the bathroom to survey the tragedy for himself. "Christ, Cliff...Have you called anyone?"

"Just... Just now found her," Cliff said, his heart racing worryingly. "Doris found her first. Amelia's in the village." Cliff made himself look down. "Norah, she's... I mean, there's no hope, is there?"

"Call 999," Tim told him, taking charge. "I'll stay here with... the body." Tim was fresh from the shower after his morning walk in the garden. He pushed black hair out of his eyes as he leaned over Norah.

"Alright. Don't let anyone else in. I'll be right back." Cliff gathered his resolve and headed downstairs to the lobby phone.

Tim could hear the call going through, Cliff's somber relaying of the events, his sadness as he told the dispatcher that CPR would be of absolutely no use at this stage. The body at his feet was Tim's first, and he found himself remembering how he'd always assumed it would be a grandparent or old neighbor, not a lovely blond woman in her twenties. Downstairs, Cliff was quiet for a moment before Tim heard him confirm the address and some other details that Tim didn't catch. Perhaps Cliff was responding to instructions about not moving the body or keeping people away until the police arrived.

"It's done, Tim. They're on their way," Cliff told him as he returned to the doorway of Norah's room. "You haven't touched anything, have you? I wouldn't want your finger-prints all over this."

"Oh, no," Tim replied. "But I want to help in any way I can. This is such a... a terrible tragedy," he said, eyes downcast.

Cliff kept his distance, staying by the bathroom door-way, while Tim stood over the body, not two feet from Norah. "I think it's better if we leave this one to the profes-sionals, don't you?" Cliff advised the younger man. "They're sure to want to interview you and our other guests." The specter of negative publicity gave Cliff an unpleasant shudder but he pushed it away, remonstrating silently with himself as he remembered that a young life had been snuffed out.

"I feel a little responsible," Tim was saying. He stared at the body again in a way that at least to Cliff in those anxious moments seemed rather odd.

"Guilt is a natural response to something like this," Cliff cautioned, shaking his head. "You had nothing to do with it, I'm sure."

"But I recommended that she stay here, you see. Norah needed a place to go. A safe place," Tim said. His eyes were fixed on the dead woman, almost as though in hope of sudden reanimation.

Cliff took a step closer to Tim. "Are you saying she was in some kind of trouble? In London?" he asked. Norah had mentioned that, like Tim, she was from the nation's capital.

Tim pursed his lips. "There was a divorce. Very messy. And the husband's not a nice character at all. He threat-ened her, followed her around. Norah needed a quiet place to collect her thoughts, figure out what to do next. I thought the *Lavender* was perfect for her. It's just," he said, welling up, "so sad that it ended this way. Do you think it was an accident? That she slipped and fell?"

Cliff watched Tim leaning over Norah's body, inspecting the terrible impact at the back of Norah's skull. "There's no way to say until the professionals get here, is there? Look, I'm going to wait in the lobby and bring them up. Please," Cliff said sincerely, "don't touch anything. I don't think you should even be in here."

But Tim was still staring at the awful wound, his eyes flitting from the basin to the bathtub, figuring out how Norah might have met her end. Tim Lloyd, investigative journalist, Cliff remembered as he descended the stairs in a strange, unpleasant fog. Tireless seeker of the truth, then. Or maybe just a juicy story.

CHAPTER SIX

CLIFF OPENED THE front door and looked up at a tall, burly police sergeant. "Thank you for coming so quickly," Cliff said. "This is just dreadful."

Sergeant Harris removed his uniform cap and stepped inside. "I'm sure it's been a difficult morning," he said in a low baritone. "But we'll take care of it. We've got one of our very best on the way here. Happens to live in Chid-dlinghurst, as a matter of fact."

Cliff showed Harris upstairs, but even before they reached the room, there was another knock at the front door. Cliff returned downstairs and opened the door. "Good morning, Mr. Swansbourne." Cliff looked up at the man standing on the doorstep. "Detective Inspector Graham."

After peering briefly at the badge which Graham held up for his inspection, Cliff said, "Yes, of course," and invited him in. The DI was in his thirties, in a grey suit, and was already scrutinizing the establishment with the air of one very much accustomed to doing so. Graham was silent for a moment as he took in details, his eyes moving quickly among the paintings by the stairs, the ornaments on the side tables, the Persian rug on the floor. The DI seemed to be absorbing the scene as though he'd be called upon later to describe its every feature.

Graham reached the top of the stairs and confirmed the basic details with Cliff. "Our housekeeper, Doris Tisbury, found her at about 9:45 this morning," Cliff reported.

"And has anyone else been in the room since then?" Graham asked, notebook open.

"Only myself and Tim Lloyd, a guest," Cliff replied. Although he felt sure that Tim had acted inappropriately, Cliff knew it was important to tell the police every detail.

DI Graham reached Norah's room and continued his careful visual survey of everything in the vicinity. Cliff watched him, finding something of the savant in the way Graham drank in the colors and shapes around him. The detective turned to look into the bathroom, noticing the same pair of shoes on the victim's feet that Doris had first seen. Beside them was Tim Lloyd, kneeling by the body, as if in the middle of carrying out his own examination.

"Sir, stand up, please!" Graham said at once. Tim paused where he was for a moment, and Graham was about to repeat the order when Tim rose, rather nonchalantly, Cliff felt, given the circumstances.

"I'd say she's been dead for about twelve hours," Tim opined, rubbing his chin.

Graham took a firm grasp of Tim's arm and led him from the bathroom. "You are Mr. Lloyd?" Graham asked.

"I am."

"You understand that this is a potential crime scene?" Graham said, his rising color the only indication that he was holding onto his temper with some effort.

"I've assisted in police investigations as part of my work. In New York," Tim explained. "As a journalist."

"A journalist. But not a medical investigator. Or a coroner. Or a police officer," Graham said mildly. He stared intently at Lloyd.

"No," Tim admitted.

"Or, indeed, as anyone remotely linked to the professional business of solving crimes."

Despite his appearance, Graham's anger was still only barely under control. If there was one thing Graham couldn't abide, it was nosy people contaminating crime scenes with their unschooled amateurism, however well-intentioned. Six months before, with less restraint than he was currently showing, Graham had flown completely off the handle, yelling into the face of a terrified volunteer who'd had the misfortune of finding the body of a missing bank teller in the woods during a massive search. Graham had initially thanked the man for his efforts—the woman had been partially buried in a remote copse and was difficult to see—but once Graham learned that the volunteer had moved strands of the woman's hair from her eyes upon finding her, he'd virtually exploded. With all the popular CSI-type shows on TV, Graham had thundered to Sergeant Harris later, you'd have thought people might have learned to keep their bloody hands to themselves.

"Return to your room, Mr. Lloyd. And stay there. Do you understand?" Tim understood and was gone in moments. After watching him leave, Graham turned to Cliff. "Mr. Swansbourne? Tell me everything you know about the deceased. Was she a regular guest?"

Cliff related what he knew and was feeling woozy enough to consider sitting on the edge of the bed, but he quickly rethought the notion in light of DI Graham's rigorous crime scene attitude. "It was her first time staying with us. A friend of Tim Lloyd, as it happens. He said something about her being recently divorced and her husband being a nasty character."

Graham's pen filled two pages of his notebook with what seemed to be Egyptian hieroglyphs but were actually a finely honed set of abbreviations combined with old-fashioned shorthand. Graham was more than a trifle behind the times in some ways, but his note-taking was far more efficient, he felt certain than typing anything into one of those tablets for which he felt considerable disdain. "Alright, then." Graham closed his notebook. "Thank you, sir. You did everything right." Cliff's reply was to give the DI a lopsided smile. "I'm going to call our pathologist, a top man, and we'll see if Mr. Lloyd's crime-fighting enthusiasm has left any trace of what might actually have killed this poor woman."

CHAPTER SEVEN

GILBERT HATFIELD—BERT to his friends—struggled simultaneously with London's Monday morning traffic and the knowledge that shedding light on whatever had befallen Norah Travis would almost certainly mean his having to miss the afternoon game. Life as a Charlton Athletic fan was tough enough without being stuck in a morgue while your team kicked off their first home game of the season.

As he gradually left the busy city streets behind, entering the far more pleasing landscape of the rural county of Surrey, the pathologist who was heading reluctantly into his sixties, negotiated the tight lanes with special care. After narrowly missing a fellow motorist who wasn't paying enough attention, he turned right, then left, then straight on at a crossroads before rolling down a gently sloping street into the almost too picturesque Chiddlinghurst. It reminded Bert of those preserved villages from the nineteenth century that were transplanted brick by brick to create a museum celebrating times past. High-end cars in driveways and the range of satellite dishes mounted as discreetly as possible on the sides of centuries-old dwellings were the only signs of encroaching modernity.

The *Lavender Inn*, for its part, could very well have been plucked from the past, its shining white paintwork, and deep black beams a pleasing contrast. And the gardens...even a person lacking green-thumbs like Bert was apt to be staggered. The planning and hundreds of hours of hard work that had gone into them were instantly obvious. It was an unfortunate fact that a guest had either chosen or been obliged to come to the end of their lives while overlooking the gardens' formal splendor.

Apparently overwhelmed—or perhaps simply understaffed—on this busy Monday morning, the local ambulance service arrived only minutes before the pathologist. Bert found them glum and feeling a little pointless as the crews sometimes did when there was so obviously nothing to be done. Mostly in these circumstances, the paramedics kept the firefighters company or talked things over with the police. This case was an exception. Everyone stood silently. DI Graham was on his own. Bert knew from experience that the police officer was waiting for him and preparing to note down as much medical data as Bert was prepared to give him.

"Still refusing to join the twenty-first century then, Detective Inspector?" Bert asked, poking fun at Graham's notebook.

Graham was in no mood to have his idiosyncrasies pointed out and gave as good as he got. "Still scraping around at the bottom of the league table?" Graham shot back, his mischievous grin proving that the DI wasn't *all* business.

Bert thumped his chest with a stern fist. "Charlton 'til I die, DI Graham, as you well know. It's just a run of bad form. They'll be back in the premiership in no time."

Graham scoffed. "Codswallop. We've got more hope of solving this one by dinner time."

At that moment Cliff Swansbourne walked up and Graham's professional center returned. He introduced the still slightly ashen innkeeper. "I want you to meet Dr. Bert Hatfield. One of the best pathologists in the business. He'll make his initial inspection of the body and the scene. We will make arrangements to move the body after that. Sergeant Harris will take photos and we'll both be conducting interviews," Graham explained to Cliff, "but then we'll be out of your hair. Another forensic crew will be along this afternoon to clean up. Standard procedure." Cliff left them to it, thankful to return to the kitchen and the routine of preparing dinner. Whether anyone would feel up to eating it was another question entirely.

Half an hour later, there was a rap at the kitchen door. "The medics are all done here, Mr. Swansbourne," Sergeant Harris said. Cliff followed him outside to where DI Graham and Bert Hatfield stood chatting. The ambulance crew slammed the back doors to their vehicle.

Cliff offered his thanks to Dr. Hatfield as the ambulance drove away. It had only been an hour since Doris had found Norah's body. Amelia had missed the entire incident. Perhaps it was better that way. With no cell phone, she had been out of reach. Cliff shuddered as he imagined the effect of a death—possibly a murder, at that—would have on her.

Bert spoke briefly with Cliff, offering condolences for the morning's tragic events and returned to his old BMW. The pathologist followed the ambulance down the winding country lanes. The area around Chiddlinghurst was an unashamedly rural part of the country, undisturbed by the spate of house-building on "greenfield" sites that had blighted the verdant areas surrounding London. Tall hedgerows flanked the lanes. Smart, green signposts gave distances to the half-mile, indicating places so tiny and hermetic that few non-locals would ever have cause to visit. The local hospital at Carrowgate was twelve miles away and just large enough to be suitable for the postmortem.

Once he got to the morgue, Bert's first tasks, as ever, were to establish the time and cause of death. With no other marks on her body except the scars from a childhood appendectomy, the blunt-force trauma to the back of Norah's skull was the leading, perhaps obvious contender for the cause of her death. Bert drew blood for toxicology screens and requested a full workup of the lab results, which would show whether Norah was pregnant, taking drugs, drunk, or poisoned.

Dr. Hatfield generally operated under guidelines that discouraged the shaving of the victim's head, but in Norah's case, it proved necessary. The impact wound was just to the right of the base of her skull, a rectangular indentation. There was another mark on her left temple; Bert suspected that she'd hit the bathtub on the way down. Using his phone, the pathologist checked his own photos of the crime scene and began to piece together the violence that had deprived the world of the lovely Norah Travis.

Computing the time of death was straightforward. Coagulation and other factors showed that at least twelve hours had passed; Norah's death had occurred late on Sunday night. Bert returned to the wound and examined it closely. There was a marking—parallel horizontal lines. He leaned closer and searched his memory for similar patterns.

It took a moment or two, but before long he was comparing the breadth and height of the wound to those of a very familiar object. Bert looked up some example dimensions online and within moments, he could say with certainty how Norah Travis had been killed, his interest in the fortunes of his beloved Charlton Athletic briefly forgotten.

CHAPTER EIGHT

SERGEANT HARRIS WAS an experienced, dedicated officer. He had long since developed an immunity to the strange, tragic fragments of life left behind when someone dies violently. But in this case, there was an unavoidable sadness. Norah Travis had been young and beautiful. If she had been murdered it was probably over nothing of any real consequence. Harris finished taking the last photos of the crime scene, and just as he was packing away his camera, Doris Tisbury appeared in the doorway. "You asked to see me, Sergeant?" she said. She was all business, with a touch of defiance in her tone from the outset.

"Yes, thanks," Harris said, far more mildly. He'd gotten further in investigations using charm and wit than he ever had with threats and intimidation. "I'm sorry you had to be the one to find Ms. Travis this morning," Harris continued. "It's never an easy thing, but you did everything right."

Doris accepted the praise gracefully. "But all the prudence in the world won't bring her back, will it?"

Harris took one more look at the spattered floor and

took his leave, beckoning for Doris to follow. They went to the room next door and took seats in the armchairs by the window. Harris brought out his tablet. "Can you tell me exactly what happened when you found Norah?" he began.

Doris relayed the events as clearly as she could. How she saw Norah's feet, worryingly still and lifeless, and then her entire prostrate body. How she quickly realized that Norah had been dead for some time. "Several hours," Doris estimated with a sad frown. "I'd say she probably lay there all night. No one to help her."

Recognizing the need to push on, Harris asked, "Did you touch or remove anything from the crime scene?"

"Of course not," Doris answered at once. "I know better than that. Watch endless police dramas on TV, I do. You know, *CSI* and all those. Love a good mystery, me."

Harris tapped the tablet. "As do I, Mrs. Tisbury."

"Besides, I don't meddle where I needn't. My back wouldn't tolerate it," Doris said, reaching for an obviously troubled spot at the base of her spine.

Harris nodded compassionately. "Only one more question, and it's just routine," he said, his usual pacifying preface for what was about to be an awkward inquiry. "Where were you between dusk yesterday and dawn this morning?"

Doris inflated slightly. "Me?"

"Just routine, like I say," Harris assured her.

"I was at home," she almost snapped. "With my husband and two of our grandchildren. We played Trivial Pursuit. Then I watched some telly with Dennis and went to bed."

"Thank you, Mrs. Tisbury. I didn't mean to intrude. I'll let you get back to your work, now."

Doris brightened quickly. "Not at all, Sergeant. You've got a job to do."

Harris stood and escorted Doris to the door. "Would you do something for me? Let Mr. Lloyd know that I'd be grateful for a minute of his time."

If Doris was a plain-spoken, straight-talking interviewee, then Tim Lloyd was as slippery as an eel. Harris found his answers evasive and short, the signs of someone with a secret. Harris thought Lloyd looked like a lawyer, maybe, or a schoolteacher, slightly pale, with that foppish black hair swinging around his eyes as his head turned. He struck Harris as nervous, maybe even just a touch guilty.

"So, when did you first meet Mrs. Travis?"

Tim blew out his cheeks. "Would you mind if we call her Norah?" he asked. His hands were fidgety, as though he were aching for a cigarette.

"When did you first meet Norah, Mr Lloyd?" Sergeant Harris repeated.

"Why do you need to know that?" In reply, Harris raised his eyebrows a tad. "We worked in the same building near Marble Arch," Tim said.

"And...? Harris prompted again.

"We got coffee from the same machine sometimes and struck up a kind of friendship."

"And how close did you become?" Harris asked. He might have put it more delicately, but he had tired of Tim's evasiveness.

"I don't know that has anything to do with..."

"Please, Mr. Lloyd," Harris said, for the third time that interview. "Just answer the question, would you?"

"We'd had coffee a few times, outside of the office," Tim explained. "But that's all."

"And you recommended that she stayed here," Harris prompted.

"Yes. The *Lavender* is my home away from home. I like to get away from the stresses of city living and my job. My parents brought me here first when I was seven, you know. Lots of memories. Besides, Amelia and Cliff are just brilliant."

"I'm sure," Harris said. "And where were you yesterday evening?"

"I had dinner with the others. The salmon was delicious. Then I went to bed."

"Were you alone, sir?"

"I don't see how that is any business of yours."

Harris sighed. "Just answer the question, sir."

Tim sniffed. "Yes, yes I was, if you must know."

"Thank you. That's all I need for now, sir. You can go."

"Look, I'm as determined as you are to find out who did this," Tim blurted. "I've worked on criminal cases before."

Harris towered over Tim. For a strange second, Tim wondered if Harris' uniform might burst open to unleash a Hulk-like, bear-monster within, but the sergeant simply glared at him. "I believe DI Graham has already given you direction on that matter."

Tim gulped slightly. "He has."

"Leave well alone," Harris said, just for a little reinforcement. Then, he was once more the helpful bobby with a solemn duty. "Thank you for your time, sir. We'll be in touch if we need you further," he said, tapping the cell phone in his breast pocket.

Harris caught up with DI Graham at the reception desk. The DI was on the phone.

"Thanks, Bert. Good work." Graham ended the call and turned to Harris. "Well, Sergeant, the postmortem is over, and the results are in. Now, who had "golf club" as their answer for the murder weapon?"

"Not me," Harris admitted, rather surprised. "Doesn't really belong in a bathroom."

Graham shrugged. "That's the thing about murder, isn't it? They never quite happen as one would prefer. For the most part, they're crimes of passion, committed suddenly and with little planning."

"Indeed, sir," Harris told him. "All we need now is to *find* the blessed thing."

CHAPTER NINE

"I'VE INTERVIEWED THE housekeeper, the one who found the body, and the other guest, Tim Lloyd. That leaves the owners. There was no one else here last night." Harris turned the guest register around to show his boss. "Just the two guest rooms were occupied, Lloyd's and the victim's. A group of seniors checked out the day before yesterday, something to do with a bowling competition."

Graham's eyebrow rose in curiosity. "Bowling? With the lanes and strikes and what have you?"

Harris saw the funny side but kept his laughter in check. It wouldn't do for Graham to believe he was being made fun of. "Crown green bowls, sir. With the little white one and the..."

"The jack," Graham told him. Harris gave him a quizzical look. "Just pulling your leg, Sergeant. My grandparents played. Got pretty good, too."

Harris checked his tablet, which seemed as indispensable to him as a pen and notepad might have been to an officer from two generations earlier. Or even one, Graham reflected. It was easy to appear a dinosaur these days if you hadn't handed over the running of your life—and the basic duties of your profession—to a couple of gadgets. As he'd explained to a young officer the other day, Graham was more "old school." The younger man had simply shrugged and returned to his phone.

"Shall we interview them together? Mr. and Mrs. Swansbourne," Harris asked.

"Let's do 'Mr.' first," Graham told him. "He was in the house when the body was found, right?"

"Right, sir."

Under their questioning, Cliff confirmed his earlier version of events and added some details including how he'd warned Tim to keep away from the body. "I also think I may have heard something as I lay in bed last night."

"From which direction did the noise come, Mr. Swansbourne?" Graham inquired.

Cliff shrugged, "I couldn't really say. Outside? Or perhaps from across the lawns, from the other side of the building where the guest rooms are. This place is quiet at the moment and noise carries. It wasn't shouting or anything untoward." Cliff blushed now. "It could even have been animals. I can't be specific. I was falling asleep. Oh, I wish I could be more helpful, Inspector," Cliff said.

Amelia was much more emphatic.

"A scream?" Graham wanted her to confirm.

"Clear as day," Amelia promised him. "From Norah's room, or close thereabouts. But I could have *sworn*," she said, fist in her palm for emphasis, "that it came right from her room."

"What kind of scream?" Harris asked.

Puzzled for a second, Amelia said, "An uncontrolled shout."

"Could it have been 'Help'?" Harris asked.

"No, I don't think so. More like, 'Aha!' Like a discovery or a surprise of some kind," she continued.

"A good surprise or a nasty one?" Graham asked.

"Hard to say," Amelia replied. "It's difficult to think of it as a happy sound, now that she's..."

Harris had learned to quickly recognize when his interviewees needed a little re-direction. "You were out in the garden, you say, when you heard the scream?"

"Yes," Amelia said. "Sunday morning's a big gardening time for me. Not that you'd be able to tell, today." She cast a rueful glance at a cluster of wayward leaves, though Harris thought the gardens damned near perfect.

"I went to her room to check if she was alright, but she opened the door as right as rain. I went away with egg on my face, none the wiser. I can't really help you any more than that."

"Alright, Mr. and Mrs. Swansbourne, thank you for your time." The police officers finished their notes and stood to take their leave.

"The gardens look spectacular," Graham told Amelia. "A real achievement."

"Thank you, but I didn't win in any of the categories at the Horticultural Society last year," Amelia remembered bitterly. She struggled to accept compliments at the best of times. And with the cloud of a murder investigation swirling around her, now wasn't the best of times at all.

Graham waved away the concern. "Those things are always fixed. It's a racket. Decades of domination by organized crime syndicates," he added with a wink. "It's like a mobster's ball."

The two police officers enjoyed watching Amelia laugh

herself silly for half a minute, all of them grateful for the welcome respite from the heaviness of their situation.

After Amelia composed herself she said, "Do you really think Norah was murdered?" Violence was an incongruity entirely unwelcome in the quiet, restrained world of the *Lavender Inn*.

"I'd say so," Graham replied. "I know it's not what you want to hear, but everything's pointing that way at the moment." Shaking her head at the callous interruption to their quiet lives, and the definitive end to another's, Amelia left the two men to their work. But something bothered Graham. "It makes me nervous," he told Harris, "when there isn't even the whiff of a suspect. Tends to mean that there's a juicy back story I haven't heard yet."

Harris saw his cue. "Should I invite Mr. Lloyd to join us again, sir?"

CHAPTER TEN

BACK IN THE guest room neighboring Norah's own, Tim Lloyd was becoming even less co-operative now that he had two officers to contend with. "Her husband wasn't a nice guy," Tim was explaining. "He wasn't good for her."

Graham let Harris do most of the talking. Harris' natural gruffness and gravity gave the questions an edge, and his tone was one that warned Tim that lying was inadvisable. "So why did Norah marry him?" Harris asked.

Tim shrugged theatrically. "There's no logic to some women, Sergeant."

"Hang on," Graham interjected. "Your earlier statement makes Norah sound like someone you occasionally had coffee with. Who knows, maybe a quick taxi back to your place to play hooky for an afternoon. And now," Graham continued, raising a silencing hand against Tim's objections, "you're an expert on her marriage, its trials and tribulations. It sounds like you were acting as some kind of amateur marriage guidance counselor."

"I never said I was an expert. She just told me a lot

about her situation, and I saw her need to get away from it all. So I recommended this place." He stopped, eyes down. "And now she's dead."

Harris gave Tim a moment before asking his next question. "What can you tell us about her husband?"

Tim took a deep breath and seemed to space out for a few seconds, glancing out of the window. Then, he spoke with sincerity. "Nasty piece of work, like I said. She should have divorced him years ago. Should never have married him in the *first* place, she sometimes said."

"Go on," Harris said, typing continuously.

"He was never happy with anything she did. Always wanted her to change her appearance, her hair, you know, always looking for the next model to upgrade to. And he's a *nobody*," Tim said, the frustration giving his voice a serrated edge, "a layabout, a benefits cheat. A con artist, and not even a very good one."

"Sounds a real charmer," Graham commented, wryly. *Also sounds like the pot calling the kettle black. After all, the towering Adonis that is Tim Lloyd is hardly catch of the day, either. Especially considering Norah's looks. She could have had any man in the world....*

"He's *scum*," Tim Lloyd told them with surprising vehemence. "I'd bet my goddamned *house* that he did this."

"Steady on there, Mr. Lloyd," Harris said. "This will go more easily if everyone remains calm." Another standard pacification line, straight from the manual, but it nearly always worked.

Graham pushed slightly away from the doorframe against which he had been leaning. "Do you play golf, Mr. Lloyd?" he asked.

"Golf?"

"Yes, sir. You know, little white ball, St. Andrews, the Ryder Cup, nineteenth hole...."

"Of course I play golf," Tim snapped. "Just about everyone who stays here does. We're right next to a great golf course. What of it?"

"Your clubs. Where are they?" Graham persisted.

"In the clubhouse," Tim told him. "Why do you ask?"

"Merely routine," Graham replied. "And a final question, Mr. Lloyd, if you don't mind. Can you account for your whereabouts on Sunday evening?"

Tim gave them both a sheepish look, and then said, "I already told your man here. I was in my own room, across the hall."

"Not with Norah, then?" Graham wanted to confirm.

Tim gave a timid shake of his head. "I was... How shall I say?" Tim said. "In the dog house. Said a couple of stupid things. All my own fault. I slept on my own, at Norah's request."

Graham jotted down his usual detailed notes and made to leave. "I see. So you confirm that you were in a relationship with the victim?"

"Well, of a sort. Not a very stable or established one, obviously." Tim looked up. "But I was trying. I'm not a cad. Norah was a very...free. And I *didn't* kill her."

"Got it. Thank you for your time, Mr. Lloyd. Sergeant, shall we?"

The two policemen walked out together, Harris closing the door behind them. It was nearly 4 p.m. and neither man had found time for lunch amid the interviews, photos, speculation, and conjecture they'd spent their day dealing with. Harris got his phone out and got directions to a pub in a neighboring village where DI Graham was less likely to be recognized, where they could mull things over in peace.

Fifteen minutes later, they found the *Fox and Fable* to be just about perfect and not at all busy. Over a quiet drink and a bowl of Mary-Anne's famous hand-cut homemade fries, the two officers weighed the case so far. They found it very thin.

"We'll have to wait until Bert tells us more about the cause of death," Graham told his colleague. "But I can tell that you're keen to pursue the jealous husband."

"I am," Harris agreed, chewing a fry, "but don't crazy ex-husbands normally beat up the new boyfriend as well?"

Graham was nodding. "He shows up, finds them together, perhaps even *in flagrante*, and then boots him out before smacking his ex-wife on the head with a golf club. Simple."

"What? Lloyd doesn't stay and defend her?" Harris argued.

"Nope, how about he turns tail and clears off, leaving the defenseless Norah to the jealous rage of the incensed husband," Graham said, continuing the thread.

"And Lloyd doesn't report the murder or call an ambulance? He just hangs out at the B&B until poor Mrs. Tisbury finds Norah the next morning?"

Graham sighed. "It's a bit thin, isn't it?"

Harris nodded. "It's a bugger. And then, for Lord knows what reason, Lloyd tramples all over the crime scene like he's some kind of amateur Sherlock-bloody-Holmes," Harris added. "Contaminating the evidence."

"Bert will be able to tell us if anything is amiss," Graham said. "He's a thorough man. I'm suspicious of Lloyd, too. Norah could have rejected him and in a fit of rage, he might have bashed her over the head. Remember how Mr. Swansbourne thought he heard noises from over in their direction?"

Harris finished his pint. "Well, first things first. We need to talk to the husband."

"Yes," Graham said, finishing his own drink. "But I don't think for a second that he'll be pleased to see us."

Harris felt his phone vibrate. "Oh, lovely jubbly," he said. "Background check on the aforementioned Mr. James Arthur Travis of picturesque Peckham in south London." Harris summarized the report for the DI. "Two convictions for driving offenses, license currently suspended owing to a second conviction for driving while intoxicated." Harris tutted like his grandmother used to. "Three arrests and two cautions for fighting in the neighborhood, one charge of assault on a police officer, later dropped. Served three months for affray and breach of the peace, but the other cases didn't go to court."

"Lovely fella," Graham said brightly. "I'll take him home next weekend to meet my mother."

Harris continued reading. "Currently address is blah-blah, phone number, you know the drill... Ah, what's this?" Harris said, tilting the phone slightly. "'Suspected involvement in the Hatton Garden jewelry heist,'" he read, eyebrows raised, "'either as an advisor or accomplice to some degree. No charges brought.' What a scintillating and varied career the young man has had. Wife stated as Norah Taylor, twenty-seven, 'estranged.'"

"They need to update that last bit," Graham added sadly. "Fancy a trip into foggy London town tomorrow, Sergeant?"

CHAPTER ELEVEN

"I SUPPOSE YOU'D better come in." The house was an identical copy of all those around it, neat but just a little box-like, with a climbing frame in the front garden and a crumbling, forgotten hosepipe propped up against the wall. The place could have used a lick of paint and looked rather forlorn under London's typically cloudy, mid-morning sky. However, Graham was careful not to judge Nikki Watkins during one of the worst weeks of her life.

"I'd like to begin," Graham said delicately as they took seats on two sofas in a living room that smelled of cigarette smoke, "by expressing our condolences, Ms. Watkins. Your sister's passing is a tragedy, and I want you to know that we're putting everything we have into finding out what happened."

Nikki was perhaps thirty, but cigarettes and cheap gin were unkindly taking their toll on her skin. She said nothing but lit a Chapman's with a big, heavy butane lighter and sat cross-legged on the couch opposite the two officers.

"We interviewed everyone at the inn, and we will be speaking with Mr. Travis this afternoon," Harris added.

Nikki gave a strange, dismissive snort and took a massive pull on her cigarette before tipping her head back and blowing a cloud of grey smoke into the smoggy air. "That bastard," she croaked. "Good-for-nothing sack of..."

"You're referring to Mr. Travis?" Sergeant Harris checked as he typed.

"Wriggled his way out of three jail sentences. Cheats on his taxes, on his benefits, the bloody lot. But no, Norah never saw that side of him, did she? Always defending him, at least when they first got together. She was always spouting some head-in-the-clouds crap about him 'having a dream,' and 'harboring ambitions.'" Nikki tutted from within her cloud of smoke. "As if that man could find his own arse with both hands, map, and a compass," she snorted. "He's a lazy, no-good little..."

Graham could have finished the rest himself. He'd interviewed hundreds of people as part of his investigations —perhaps over a thousand, by now—and there was always that one character in the tale who had never endeared himself to the others, the one who was the object of derision, the perpetual disappointment, the one who'd let himself down or kept the wrong company. Most often a young man, he was the one who everyone always assumed would "never amount to anything."

"Ms. Watkins, could you shed some light on their relationship? Norah seems to have stayed with him far longer than many would have." Graham was doing his delicate best, but there was no subtle way of asking what many must have wondered. *How did a total loser like Travis snag a blond bombshell like Norah?*

"They married young. Too young," Nikki told them.

"She wanted away from our parents, bless them, and Travis promised that he was on the up-and-up, that they'd be traveling around the French Riviera, or shopping in New York. And she swallowed it!" Nikki exclaimed, still amazed that her sister could have been quite so gullible. "After two years of marital 'bliss,' she finally woke up and smelled the coffee. Finally, Norah recognized what we all knew—that he was just a sham. No prospects, no education. Just a career criminal, waiting for his big break."

Harris typed quickly, while Graham made shorter, hieroglyphic notes in his notepad.

"But he couldn't even get criming right," Nikki commented bitterly. "'He was always getting caught or was a suspect and had to lie low. Any number of times," she recalled. "Chronic underachiever, even when he was on the wrong side of the law."

Graham made another note and then said, "Actually, Ms. Watkins, we prefer our criminals incompetent and bumbling. Makes them a lot easier to catch," he smiled.

"Well, he got caught alright, but nothing stuck. Eventually, Norah saw the writing on the wall and decided against spending three or four years visiting that useless nobody in jail, trying to keep it together on the outside while he relaxed in some daycare for the unforgivably stupid, and she walked. Not before time, neither."

Harris raised an eyebrow to the DI, who returned his glance. "What we're really trying to decide," Graham explained, "is whether Mr. Travis should be considered a suspect."

Nikki knocked ash down her black t-shirt in a fit of throaty laughter. "*Suspect?*" she wheezed. "He's *got* to be a *suspect*! Who the hell *else* would have done something like this?"

"We're having the same suspicions that you are, Ms. Watkins, but until we can prove it beyond a reasonable doubt, Mr. Travis remains a person of interest in this case," Graham explained, "but not yet a *suspect*."

Nikki almost spat her next words. "Think whatever you want. Do your interviews, get your lab boffins on it, analyze his DNA and his fingerprints, and what have you. But I *know*, right now, sitting here, that he lost control. He couldn't handle her leaving him. Failure in business, in school, in crime, and now in his marriage, too."

"What made her finally leave?" Harris asked.

Nikki was reluctant now. "Couldn't say," she shrugged, suddenly appearing reluctant to trash talk her ex-brother-in-law.

"I think you can, Ms. Watkins," Graham said with as much gentle encouragement as he could, "and even if you don't think it's relevant, or you aren't certain it's true, it might help us."

Nikki reached for a cigarette before realizing she already had one smoldering between her yellowed fingers. She inhaled the last quarter-inch of tobacco with the enthusiasm of one enjoying a pleasure unlikely ever to be repeated, then let the smoke escape in a slightly gray cloud of noxious fumes. She reached for her next cigarette before she'd stubbed the previous one out.

"She was seeing a man. A nice man," she said mildly. "Worked near her office in Marble Arch, I think he did."

His fingers traveling at speed across the screen of his tablet, Harris asked, "Was his name, Tim?"

"Yeah." Nikki paused. She tilted her head slightly. "He's not caught up in this, is he?"

"What can you tell us about him?" Graham asked.

"I only met him once. Seemed nice. Certainly a darn

sight better than that worthless ex-husband of hers," Nikki said venomously. "Norah talked about going on away with him. Just as a friend, she said."

"Did her ex know about Norah's friendship with Tim?"

Nikki stubbed out her second cigarette without taking a drag and put the ashtray aside. "No, I don't reckon he knew. But, you know what? Travis was clueless about her. Just assumed that he was the center of her world, just like he was the center of his own. I think he might actually have been stupid enough to believe that Norah would come back to him, even after everything." Nikki shook her head incredulously. "I mean, he broke their wedding vows before their first anniversary. Saw other women, hit her... She had bruises one night, not three months after marrying. I told her to call the police, but would she?"

Harris fielded this one. "Did she ever report him? We always encourage victims of domestic violence to come forward, Ms. Watkins."

Another derisive snort. "And what the bleedin' hell do you reckon old Jimmy would have made of *that*?" she demanded. "Her life wouldn't have been worth living!"

Graham followed the thread a little further. "Do you think Norah wanted to come to the police, and perhaps her husband threatened her?"

Nikki leaned against the back of the sofa. "I couldn't say. They fought like cats and dogs, but they were man and wife, you know what I mean? She had a weird loyalty towards him. She used to say, 'When you're married you love together, you fight together, and if the time comes, you go down together.'"

Her words reminded Harris of something a marriage counselor had once said during the first separation from his wife, Judith: "A marriage takes two. One won't do."

"I don't think she would have ever grassed on him," Nikki continued. "Nah, I reckon he lost it one night and went down to see her. Her having a separate life wouldn't have sat well with him. Things probably got out of hand." Nikki's face turned mulish and she crossed her arms. "You must find him, bring him down."

As the two men left, Nikki looked pale and upset. She had that look in her eye which Harris and Graham had both seen too often. It was the pain of loss, sudden, irreversible, and impossibly hard to bear, one which would go on hurting and nagging and gnawing for years.

In Graham's experience, the only thing that even *began* to assuage that kind of pain was seeing the person responsible for it in the dock and subsequently convicted and sentenced. The perpetrator doomed to years of incarcerated misery offered a form of karmic wiping of the slate and only then could the person lost be grieved over. Understanding this gave Graham an edge, an oddly emotional resolve, a steely determination. He would find that closure for Nikki. For her and for himself, he'd find the killer, whoever it was.

CHAPTER TWELVE

"£225,000" HARRIS COUNTERED.

"Give over," Graham said. "You can't ask more than £210,000 for that."

"Alright, what about this one?" Harris pointed to another brick home as they drove slowly down the street. They were looking for number eighty-eight.

Graham evaluated the house, as they often did on streets like this. "Needs new guttering, yard isn't all that great. Say, £205,000?"

Harris played his part in their ongoing joust about London's outrageous property prices. "Two *hundred*," he let the gigantic sum sink in, "and five *thousand* pounds?"

"I'd say," Graham said.

"For *that?* We're not in sodding Kensington, you know," Harris reminded him.

"It's not falling down or anything. £205,000 sounds reasonable."

"Jesus, but this one really *is* falling down," Harris muttered as they pulled up outside number eighty-eight.

"Drags down the whole neighborhood. What would you pay?"

Graham made a face. "£160,000 or so, but you'd be buying it for the land and starting again."

"I think we can take it that Mr. Travis is not a man given to spontaneous bouts of home improvement," Harris concluded. Then he grinned at his boss. "See, I'll make detective any day now."

James Travis had made his home in what was by far the less pleasant half of a semidetached dwelling, perhaps two miles from his sister-in-law's address and uncomfortably close to one of the main rail lines that brought commuters in from the south. The front yard was a scramble of limp, tangled grass, and detritus—a discarded child's bicycle with only one wheel, well-chewed dog bones, and a blue and red garden gnome which looked as though it was someone's favorite air rifle target. Graham knocked on the door where the green paint had flaked away.

"Good afternoon," Graham said as the door swung open. "Would you be Mr. Travis?"

Standing in the doorway was a shirtless, skinny man of around thirty-five. He had short blond hair and an unimpressed, sneering expression. "Eh?"

"I'm Detective Inspector Graham, sir. This is Sergeant Harris. We'd like to ask you a few questions."

"What about?" Travis asked defiantly.

Your ex-wife, who died violently not two days ago, you pig-ignorant troglodyte. "We're investigating the death of Norah Travis, sir. You spoke with one of my London-based colleagues this morning. I was at the crime scene in Chiddlinghurst yesterday," Graham said.

"And what?" Travis demanded. "You think I went down there and murdered her?"

Graham cleared his throat. "Could we speak inside please, Mr. Travis?"

"Why?"

The defiant tone, Travis's slovenly appearance, and the lamentable state of the place were all useful data points for Graham. On their own, they might not implicate James Travis in the murder of his ex-wife but they offered clues to the character of the man. Anyone with a nose, a sense of social justice, or an enthusiasm for human compassion would have found Jimmy repugnant. He was like a lobotomized skinhead on poppers. But Graham had learned long ago that everyone has a rich inner life, an invisible counterpart to the aspect of themselves they showed to the public. Although he may appear one way now, James Travis was almost certainly more complicated than his bony, vaguely anarchistic exterior might suggest. To uncover whether that interior was laudable was Graham's mission.

"This isn't a conversation you want to have on your doorstep, sir, what with all the neighbors seeing. May we?" It wasn't a true question and Harris all but barged past Travis into the house. Like Nikki's, it smelled of cigarettes and also burned toast with an aesthetic appeal that was but a single notch above a crack den in Graham's view.

"When did you last see your ex-wife, Mr. Travis?" Graham asked once they were all seated around the kitchen table. Sitting in the living room would have necessitated two hours of assiduous cleaning.

"Can't remember," Travis answered. "It's been ages. Got no idea where she's been sleeping or anything."

Harris tried something. "We are sorry for your loss, Mr. Travis. This is a tragedy."

"Eh?" Travis had still not located a shirt nor offered the officers anything to drink. "Tragedy? Yeah, sure, mate. Call it whatever you want. But for me, she was a pain in the arse when we married, and she's been a pain in the arse ever since," he whined.

The two policemen exchanged a glance. "Can you account for your whereabouts on Sunday night, sir?" Harris asked.

"Hackney. With a bunch of my friends. Got the last bus back at about three in the mornin'," Travis told them.

Graham asked next, "Do you play golf, by any chance?"

A skeptical look jarred Travis' face. "Do I do *what?*"

For the second time since the investigation began, Graham prepared to explain the basics of a globally popular sport. "Golf, you know, with the clubs and the ball."

"No, Detective chief whatever-your-name-is, I don't play bloody golf. That's for posh geezers, innit? Do I look like I'm bloody posh?"

Graham let Harris ask the rest of the basic interview questions while he poked around the house. He found nothing to interest him. Travis appeared to be on the inside exactly who he said he was on the outside—a scruffy layabout with low-level criminal tendencies. When they returned to their car, Graham gave Harris directions back to Chiddlinghurst and explained his theory.

"We'll get the Hackney lot to check out Jimmy's alibis, but I'll tell you right now that I don't think he killed Norah."

Harris glanced over at his boss. "Really?"

"Bet you a hundred quid. Oh, he was glad to be rid of her," Graham noted, "but nothing about him, however unpleasant and cave-dwelling he might appear, shouted 'murderer' to me. And I've met more than my share. He's not resourceful enough to negotiate his way to the Home Counties of his own volition, murder someone in an unfamiliar place, set up an alibi, and put on that performance of innocence. He's way too limited."

"So, there's something else going on here besides the jealous husband and the ex-wife with the new boyfriend," Harris observed.

"Could it have been Tim Lloyd?" Graham wondered to himself. "And, if so, why?" he said next, staring out at the traffic. Rain began to fall, light but persistent.

"Or, to ask it another way, sir, why would Tim kill her and then hang around the hotel for the next twelve hours so the local constabulary could interview him as part of a murder investigation? What advantage was there to staying, once the deed was done?" Harris changed lanes to pass a bus full of teenagers, some of whom entertained themselves during their journey by giving the officers a two-fingered salute.

"To maintain the impression of innocence," Graham said, ignoring the unruly teens, "We always imagine that the killer strikes and then flees the scene. But more often than you'd think, the murderer stays around, gathers information, and tries to blend in. Some criminals get a kick out of watching the enormous amount of fuss their crimes generate. It's why they often revisit the scene of the crime."

Harris thought it over. "Do you see Tim Lloyd as the type to kill someone and then be cool enough to stick around?"

"I don't. But I also don't love the theory which implies that the murderer walked in off the street, clubbed Norah over the head, and then vanished. I mean, there are such things as contract killings, but they're exceptionally rare and seem implausible in this instance."

Harris nodded. "And I don't see Mr. Travis stumping up a couple of grand for someone to bump off his wife."

"Not even for a minute," Graham agreed. His phone rang. "It's Bert. You know where to turn, right? Junction eleven." Harris nodded and Graham took the call. "Hello Bert, what's the good news?" Graham listened for a minute, thanked the pathologist, and hung up. "He's identified our murder weapon."

"Wait, what? We already know it was a golf club!" Harris asked, confused.

"No, sorry, I mean Bert knows what *kind* of golf club it was."

"Ah," Harris said.

"It was a driver." DI Graham made another note in his book. "Big, powerful. Ideal for knocking down a defenseless woman and taking her out."

"Could it have been wielded by another woman?" Harris said.

"Who, Amelia? What possible motive could she have?"

"Or Doris?" the sergeant tried next. "Decides she's fed up with people leaving their dirty towels on the floor," he said, affecting Doris' Northern accent.

"Be serious, Sergeant," Graham said mildly. "Besides, Doris has a gold-plated alibi."

"Well, bugger," Harris said, deflated.

"Indeed," Graham agreed.

CHAPTER THIRTEEN

DUSK WAS SETTLING on the village of Chiddlinghurst when the two officers arrived back. They made straight for the *Lavender*, parking the police car in the gravel driveway at the front. Graham always felt a little self-conscious about showing up in such a highly visible police vehicle, but his own unmarked Audi was in London. He justified his misgivings on the basis that it was reasonable to think that the public gained security and confidence from seeing the badge of the constabulary, especially just after a gruesome and unexpected murder right in their midst.

Cliff Swansbourne greeted them at the door. "Welcome back, travelers. Did you find answers in London?"

Graham shed his suit jacket and loosened his tie. "Somewhat, Mr. Swansbourne. Could we bother you for a cup of tea?"

"Of course," Cliff replied, but then seemed to beckon slightly for the two men to follow him. "Got a couple of details I wanted to pass on," he whispered. "Things that might help your investigation, you know?"

They retreated into the kitchen, which seemed a little overly cautious to Graham, seeing as the inn was virtually empty. "You've already been very helpful, Mr. Swansbourne," Graham was saying. "It can't have been easy..."

"Tim Lloyd," Cliff said without further preparation. "I had a word with him earlier today, while you were in town." Cliff tossed a tea bag into a remarkably ancient teapot and followed it with boiling water. "Amelia was there too, but she's visiting her sister tonight. Every Tuesday evening, without fail. Murder investigation or none."

"Nothing more important than family," Sergeant Harris contributed, then winced slightly.

Graham took the offered mug of tea. "What did Mr. Lloyd have to say? Please be precise. I'm sure I don't have to remind you," he said, reaching for his notebook, "of the seriousness of this matter. You must relay everything he said, word for word if you can."

Cliff was nodding. "It's just that... Well, we've known Tim since the first week we took over the place. He loves it here. Home away from home, all of that. He's never caused any trouble, except maybe just occasionally being a little too familiar. I mean, we're hoteliers, not his family, though he's been very kind and a very regular guest. Amelia indulges him, you see," Cliff explained, turning to Harris. "She's got a soft spot for him. In fact, she told me not to pass any of this on, but I just have to..."

With a flat palm extended, Graham said gently, "Take your time, sir. These things are always easier if you take a couple of deep breaths first."

Cliff followed his advice. Graham and Harris could easily see that this unwelcome case had brought with it more stress and distraction than Swansbourne was ready to cope with. Not only had there been a death in their inn, but a *bone fide* murder. An accident or a heart attack would have been one thing, but this meant that someone had stolen into their quiet, rural establishment and beaten a woman to *death* with a golf club. It would have been hard on anyone, but Graham had the sense that Cliff Swansbourne, for all his maturity and experience, might not be built from the sternest stuff.

"I went to speak to him," Cliff confided. "I was upset with him for his behavior yesterday morning. You know, hanging around the crime scene like that, poking his nose in. I thought you were going to tear him to bits when you found him with the body, Detective. Would have served him right, too."

"Simply trying to maintain the integrity of the scene," Graham explained.

"Well, I told him I didn't think he should have been there, nosing around. And do you know what he said? He told me, as God is my witness that he and Norah were very close. 'Closer than any of you think,' he told me. They were planning to head off to the Caribbean together in a couple of days, for heaven's sake! Hadn't told anyone! We thought Norah was staying at least through the end of the week."

Harris was typing, Graham was writing, and Cliff seemed more unburdened with each passing moment. This information had clearly weighed on him.

"Well, as you know," Graham clarified, "he told us that they were on friendly terms, the occasional coffee, perhaps something more intimate. But going on holiday together—that's a new piece of information."

"I mean," Cliff said, "I'd always assumed he was trustworthy but he lied about how close they were, and for no good reason that I can see. Can we trust him, even now?" Cliff asked them.

"Mr. Swansbourne," Graham began, "we'll speak with Mr. Lloyd again in the light of this new information."

"But why not just tell us everything?" Cliff wondered aloud. "Who cares if he was in love with Norah, or about to jet off somewhere with her? She's divorced, he's single. It's the twenty-first century," he marveled. "We've got men marrying men and women marrying women, bless them all. It's a much more tolerant society than the one I grew up in. Why would Tim lie about a straightforward relationship? What can he be hiding?"

"You're making some good points, sir," Graham told Cliff. "We'll be speaking with Mr. Lloyd some more, rest assured."

"I just want to be as useful as possible," Cliff explained. "You know, the faster this is resolved, the faster we can put the whole nasty episode behind us. It's made us both re-think whether," Cliff said, his eyes welling slightly as he glanced around the kitchen, "we really, truly want to be here."

Harris contributed his two cents. "Anyone would understand that, sir," he said, handing back his empty tea mug, "but it would be a great shame if a cowardly act like this ended up changing the direction you're taking. I mean, your reviews are all five-star, and the gardens look incredible..."

"Amelia's doing, I assure you," Cliff said. "She could run this place with one hand tied behind her back. Put her and Doris Tisbury together and literally, anything becomes possible."

Silently, broodingly, DI Graham let a thought percolate up into his consciousness and, for the first time, receive genuine and careful thought: *Capable of anything... Including murder?*

He put the thought aside for the moment, along with a raft of other theories. "With our interviews complete," Graham said, "barring one more little chat with Mr. Lloyd, we'd like to move onto the forensic stage."

Cliff frowned. This sounded immediately like more disruption, more police presence, more pathologists and scientists busying themselves in his well-kept hallways. "I thought Norah's body was over at the morgue, you know, for the examination."

"It is," Graham confirmed. "But we've got a strong lead on a murder weapon."

Cliff brightened. "Oh? That's good news. And so *quickly*." He marveled again at the pace of change. "Guess you're just as good as those detectives on TV."

I'm a darn sight better than that fictional shower of incompetence. And I'm still getting warmed up. Graham let the remark pass. "Do you have any golf clubs on the premises?"

"Yes, of course. A number of our regular guests leave their sets here in-between visits. They prefer that to carting them back and forth, you know."

"We'll be needing access to every single one, if you don't mind," Graham informed Cliff.

After another long frown and a surprised shake of the head, Cliff said, "But there are over a *dozen* of our guests' golf bags in the shed. You need to search through all of them?"

"In actual fact," Graham told him, "we'll only be examining the drivers in detail, and the rest more superficially. But there's a strong chance that the murder weapon is among them."

"Well, of course. Whatever you need."

"We'll make a start first thing," Graham promised him.

"The local Scenes of Crime lads are very efficient. They'll be here for the morning, I imagine, but by lunchtime, we should be out of your hair."

Cliff saw the two men to their car and then returned to the kitchen table. *Perhaps it really is time to pack this in. Sell the murder story as some salacious piece of gossip to a glossy magazine, get a handsome check, and retire for good. Sun, sand, and margaritas.* Right then, at the end of a long and horrid day, it sounded as good as it ever had.

CHAPTER FOURTEEN

CHRIS STEVENS WAS the Scenes of Crime Officer on duty, an energetic and thoroughly professional man with a thin, black mustache and almost famously nerdy glasses. Universally respected for his work but not celebrated for his sense of humor, Stevens was in a bullish, problem-solving mood as he strode down the hallway of the *Lavender*. He began sizing up the murder scene within moments of his arrival, just after eight on this promisingly sunny Wednesday morning.

"There's always contamination of some kind," he explained to the small crowd which gathered outside the room—the Swansbournes, DI Graham, and Sergeant Harris.

Amelia was watching these events with interest, but if she were honest, she would have rather that the bunch of them finished their work and disappeared. She liked DI Graham well enough, and the burly sergeant was nice and very professional; if there *had* to be a murder investigation at the *Lavender*, this cast of characters was as discreet and helpful as she could have hoped for. But their uniforms and medical bags, the paraphernalia of police work and evidence gathering... these things didn't *belong* here. They were an unwelcome reminder that mere yards from where she and Cliff slept, something utterly terrible had happened.

The next to arrive was a curious but frustrated Doris Tisbury, whose sole hope for the day was to finally clean the murdered woman's room. Something about the incompleteness of her task genuinely bothered Doris, as though the murder scene were a missing piece from her personal jigsaw, and only her prompt and thorough attention would bring her mind some rest. Her son, a schoolteacher and certainly no medical expert, had "diagnosed" Doris with "OCD" or some such, and it drove her batty to hear him carry on about "reward circuits" and "habituated compulsions" that she knew nothing about, but which were clearly directed at her. Back in the day, Doris informed her son testily, neatness was considered a virtue, not frowned upon as something requiring treatment by a psychiatrist or worse. Not for the first time, she considered that she'd been born in the wrong century.

"Mr. Lloyd isn't up yet, I don't think," Cliff told Stevens as the bespectacled forensic scientist located his swabs and a camera. "But he was the only one, besides Doris, who was in here before the police arrived."

Cliff and Amelia kept their distance as Stevens began taking a swab from the floor by the bathtub. "I'll need a DNA sample from him and from Doris. Hopefully, our killer left some small fragment of himself behind."

"Or herself," Amelia added.

Stevens straightened up and slotted the swab away in its plastic tube. "You know how many murders there are by golf club every year in the UK?" he asked.

Amelia bristled. She wasn't sure she liked this officious young man with his know-it-all air. "I'm sure you'll enlighten me."

"Somewhere around none," the SOCO told her. "It's an extremely uncommon murder method. I can only think of two, historically, and they were all *ages* ago. Men committed both of them. In fact, the vast majority of murders ultimately prove to have a male perpetrator," he added. "Particularly those involving clubs, bats, sticks, or other methods of beating a victim to death."

Cliff attempted to lighten the atmosphere. "I don't know, Mr. Stevens. In the hands of our Doris, I'm sure a golf club could lay waste to nations."

Doris loved this kind of banter and gave as good as she got. "Not me," she said, picking up fresh towels from her cart and heading down the hallway. "I'm a lover, not a fighter."

Cliff cracked up laughing as the big-framed Doris marched off to her daily chores. It was the first time he could remember laughing—or even *smiling*—since Doris had first delivered the terrible news.

"Well," Amelia said, close to a fit of the giggles herself and grateful for a little light relief from the heaviness that had blanketed their days since Norah's body had been found. "There's an image to conjure with."

"I'd rather not," Cliff managed through his laughter.

Stevens ignored the entire exchange and silently wished for some time alone. There were always curious onlookers, and Stevens didn't mind in principle, but they invariably found cause to contribute some theory or other which was apt to knock Stevens off his stride. He was a scientist, not an investigator, and he simply wanted to collect evidence before feeding it into DI Graham's investigative process. Besides, it was to be a busy morning, even once he'd finished with this blood-stained bathroom floor.

Around thirty minutes later, Cliff showed Stevens to the shed and opened the door. There was that reassuring, slightly musty odor of leather and metal emanating from the interior as the door creaked open. Cliff had been offering guests inexpensive, secure golf club storage since he and Amelia had taken over the *Lavender*. It made economic sense. The only costs were a new lock and a motion-detector system for the back garden. There was one problem, however. A family of foxes who lived in the countryside beyond the village visited regularly. They would set off all the security lights as they trotted brazenly through at night. On occasion, guests complained bitterly to Amelia and Cliff about being woken by a blast of bright light invading their bedrooms in the middle of the night. Cliff's response was to produce his phone and show a video of the cheeky culprits and their kits gamboling across the lawn. The guests would inevitably pipe down, charmed at the sight. And so, thanks to the storage shed, Cliff made some easy money that allowed him a quality of wine a notch above that he would have drunk otherwise. Easy money was one of Cliff's favorite things.

Cliff was about to pull bags full of clubs out onto the grass for Stevens' inspection before the SOCO let him know, a tad too brusquely for Cliff's own tastes, that he'd need to inspect each club in situ.

"We mustn't compromise the scene, sir. We must protect it. Even if the murder weapon isn't here, if the killer touched a bag, for example, we might get a partial print off the leather." Cliff backed off to watch the thirty-something Stevens do his work. "My first task is to search for what *isn't* there," he said. "If the murderer took their weapon from this shed and abandoned it elsewhere, there'll be a driver missing."

A few minutes later, careful tallying of the clubs showed Stevens that not a single golf bag lacked a driver. "All present and correct," he muttered.

"So now what?" Cliff asked.

Without answering, Stevens pulled out his forensics kit. It surprised Cliff to see that the SOCO carried his equipment in a backpack as though he were a college student. Cliff had been expecting some kind of futuristic tool bag. In his imagination, it glowed blue neon and jetted out steam when it was opened. Stevens didn't even carry one of those natty, black leather bags, like a country doctor from the 1950s. In Cliff's view, a backpack was prosaic by comparison. "Now," Stevens told him, "I meticulously swab every golf club, starting with the drivers, to see if there are any bloodstains."

"And if there are?" Cliff wanted to know.

Stevens enjoyed appearing an expert in front of laymen but did not possess the insight to realize that by doing so he encouraged their questions, questions he didn't appreciate. Stevens could be

chippy at the best of times, curmudgeonly at worst, but he kept his resentment at Cliff's interruption from his expression. A sigh and a slightly curt tone were the only indications of his predilection not to suffer fools easily. "Then we'll probably have found the murder weapon. Unless the denizens of the local golf courses are given to smearing blood on their clubs as part of some gruesome and ancient hazing ritual," he said. It was the closest thing to a joke Stevens had uttered since he'd arrived, a record which would stand all day.

CHAPTER FIFTEEN

"WELL THEN, I'LL leave you to it." Cliff started to leave, a nice cup of tea and a bacon sandwich firmly on his mind, when an old man appeared next to the shed.

"Morning, there, Clifford!" the man said, his overly loud tone hinting at his deafness. Bob Sykes was one of those men who had been very old for a very long time. If Cliff were pressed, he'd have guessed Sykes was pushing ninety, but the man himself claimed to have long since forgotten. "Old age," he was fond of saying, "always comes at a bad time." Despite his vintage, Sykes was a groundskeeper at the nearby golf course.

"Morning, Mr. Sykes," Cliff responded. There wasn't a person in Chiddlinghurst who would dream of referring to Mr. Sykes by his first name. Cliff handled the introductions between Sykes and Stevens.

"Now what's this I hear," Sykes asked, his voice a reedy tenor, "about a pretty lady coming to grief in one of your bathrooms?"

"I'm afraid we've had a murder, Mr. Sykes," Stevens

explained. "We're investigating exactly what happened, and we're getting closer every hour."

Sykes leaned on a weather-beaten golf club. "Well, I heard about it, and it's a rotten thing to happen, ain't that right, Clifford?"

"Damned tragedy," Cliff told him.

"I says to the wife," Sykes related, "I says, 'A murder at the *Lavender*? Never in a million years. There's scarce ever trouble with the Swansbournes,' I told her."

The stress of the past few days and the inevitable damage to the *Lavender*'s reputation showed momentarily on Cliff's lined face. "Well, it's poor Norah I feel sorry for," he said finally. "We'll muddle along alright, but she's...."

"In a far better place," Sykes said, curling a bony finger toward the sky. "Mark my words, Clifford. Far better and more beautiful than any place we've ever seen with these mortal eyes."

Stevens raised his head from his work. "I'd like to believe that."

"Are you getting spiritual in your advanced years Mr. Sykes?" Cliff asked.

The old man cackled. "Wait 'til you're as old as I am," he told Cliff. "Spend a moment staring mortality and eternity in the face and then tell me there's no splendor or comfort to be found in a vision of the celestial city. There's power in that message, young 'uns, I tell you."

"Or perhaps," Cliff said, "you're squaring things with the Divine before you shuffle off to meet him."

Another cackle. Sykes sounded like an ancient witch when he laughed. "It certainly wouldn't do," the old man said, "for me to get all the way to the Pearly Gates and find my name's not on the list." He leaned once more on the golf club and only then looked down at it with a spark of realization in his eyes. "Well, I'll be a monkey's uncle. I was nothing more than a hair's breadth from forgetting what I came over to say!"

"What's that, Mr. Sykes?" Cliff asked. His bacon sandwich daydream had receded alarmingly, and he was keen to get it back on track.

"I found this driver in the bunker on the fourteenth," he said, lifting the club on which he'd been leaning. "Wondered if one of your guests had forgotten it. Funny place to have a driver out, wouldn't you say? The middle of the fairway, with bunkers all around?"

Cliff wisely decided not to touch the driver but motioned to Stevens, who took it between gloved thumbs and forefingers as though it were a holy relic. "Where precisely was this found, Mr. Sykes?" Stevens said, excitement in his voice.

"Half-buried, it was," Sykes reported. "Like someone tried to hide it there, and either did a rotten job or someone else dug it up part of the way. I found it sticking out of the bunker, like a bit of old shrapnel on a beach."

"And when did you make this discovery?" Stevens asked, already preparing to swab the metal where the club would meet the ball. *Or the back of Norah Travis' head.*

"Not an hour ago," Sykes replied. "My first thought was that somebody had forgotten it, but then I thought of you. I got myself wondering if one of you policemen might like to have a look at it. There was word going around the pub last night that the young woman was hit over the head with a golf club. That was the rumor, anyway, unless my old hearing let me down again. Of all the sorry ways to meet your maker...."

"No, you're quite right," Stevens said. "We're confident the murder weapon was a driver."

"Well," Sykes said, "I'm relieved not to be entirely losing my marbles."

Stevens gave Cliff a meaningful glance and then reached for his cell phone. "DI Graham?" he confirmed. "Chris Stevens, SOCO... Yes, I'm in the shed in the back garden." He glanced at Sykes who grimaced comically, enjoying the moment. "I've got a local resident here, groundskeeper at the golf club. And the thing is, sir, I'm pretty sure he's brought me the weapon that was used to murder Norah Travis."

CHAPTER SIXTEEN

LOUISE HOVERED NERVOUSLY by the doorway to the crime lab as if afraid of being accused of trespass. Or, as her boss sometimes called it, "lurking." She was always hesitant to disturb Bert Hatfield when he was in one of his "beautiful mind" moods. The largest whiteboard she had found in the office supply catalog covered one wall of the lab and Bert had spent the first hour of this Thursday morning scribbling on it with zest and purpose.

"Er, sir?" Louise tried, tapping tentatively at the door frame.

Bert didn't miss a beat, his marker squeaking noisily on the board. "Louise, my dear, if I've told you once, I've told you a thousand times. My colleagues call me Bert," he explained, still writing, "and you're my colleague."

"Yes, sir."

There was another animated squeak. "Oh, for pity's sake," he said with a reassuring smile. "With what can I help you, oh timid shrew?"

Lurking—yes, that was the word—immediately behind Louise was an even more reluctant figure, a teenager in a smart grey and black school uniform.

"Bloody hell," Bert exclaimed, finally capping the pen and slotting it onto the board's metal rail and peering at the schoolgirl. "Do they still make you wear those ghastly things?"

Louise found her voice once more. "This is Fiona. From St. Aidan's." The silence betrayed Bert's having entirely forgotten about this long-planned work experience visit. "It was in your calendar," Louise added.

"Bugger," the pathologist muttered. "Quite alright, quite alright. Come on in, Fiona. Sorry about all that." He ushered her into the room and politely dismissed Louise who returned to her front desk duties. "You've arrived on a rather auspicious day, as it happens."

"Really?" the fifteen-year-old asked. She had bright blue eyes and a quiet curiosity which Bert found both pleasant and rather admirable, particularly given that his lab dealt almost exclusively with the lamentable and gruesome.

"You'll have heard about the murder over in Chiddlinghurst?" he asked, leading Fiona around two tables stacked high with books and papers toward his desk in the corner. In truth, there could have laid almost anything under the tremendous weight of documentation Bert had accrued and "stored." It gave the lab the feel of a much loved but slightly shabby library whose main topic was death: manners of bringing it about, and the people guilty of having done so.

"Norah Travis," Fiona replied crisply. "Very sad. Only twenty-seven, wasn't she?"

"Well done for reading the news," Bert told her. "I didn't think young people bothered with it."

Fiona was not, as Bert would find during a memorable morning, a typical fifteen-year-old. She had bent over backward to be assigned this rather special position, writing letters and using her father's modest influence as a human resources manager for a local pharmaceutical company. To be a pathologist had been her dream since childhood, and she had little interest in any other career. Hers was no morbid fascination with death, however. She was passionate about the *process*, the hard science of sleuthing one's way from complete confusion to stand-up-in-court certainty. She wanted to catch bad people, of course, and bring closure to families, but her focus had always been on *how* a murderer was brought to justice. "It just revs me up," she had explained to a slightly perplexed career counselor at her school. "I can't explain it."

"I read the news all the time," Fiona reported honestly. "Are you working on evidence connected to her case?" A flash of excitement accompanied Fiona's question. *I might help solve a murder! On my first day!*

"I am," Bert reported. "We've had a couple of strokes of luck, but we're not there yet."

He opened three different files on the computer and allowed Fiona to read them. She did so quickly, perched on a black stool by Bert's desk, taking notes on a spiral-bound pad. Then Bert had a thought.

"You've signed all the non-disclosure stuff, right?" Fiona nodded. "Good. Because you really can't discuss any of this with anyone. Not until we've taken the case to court. Alright with you?"

"You can trust me," Fiona said. Bert believed her at once. There were some people you just knew wouldn't let you down.

Once Fiona had finished reading and taking her notes, Bert filled her in on the rest.

"Thankfully, we're blessed with a gifted SOCO. You know what one of those is, don't you?"

"Scenes of Crime Officer," Fiona replied.

"Good girl. Now, our man Stevens is very thorough, really one of the best. With his help," Bert said, reaching across to an object wrapped in plastic, "and a lucky break, something has fallen into our laps. Care to identify it?"

Fiona took the golf club in her hands as though being handed a piece of the original Cross. "I don't play golf, so I don't know what type. But it seems heavy," she said, weighing the thick-handled club in her hands.

"It's a driver," Bert said. "Heaviest of the lot. If someone raised this and brought it down," he said, mimicking the motion, "or swung from the side, they'd cause a serious injury, wouldn't you say?"

Fiona tried swinging the club in an imitation of the murderous impact. "Fractures, for sure," she said.

"Now," Bert said, taking back the club. "We've got a theory that Norah Travis was hit, very hard just the once, by a golf club. See here," he said, returning to the computer screen and bringing up images from the postmortem. "Notice this pattern of crossed lines? They're different in every manufacturer, of course."

"And this pattern," Fiona said, almost touching the screen, "matches the club the SOCO found?"

She was brimming with an excitement kept under control only by the severity of the case and the gravity of her surroundings. Before this moment, Fiona would never have dared believe that she'd be allowed even to *see* this lab, never mind examine the evidence under scrutiny. She was on cloud nine.

"It does. Within tolerances. But there's a way we can make sure, and that's how I was going to spend my morning," Bert said, giving her an almost conspiratorial grin. "Care to join me?"

CHAPTER SEVENTEEN

DETECTIVE INSPECTOR GRAHAM sat rather gloomily in the dining room of the *Lavender* bed-and-breakfast at just after 9 a.m. on this promisingly bright Thursday. He was not, by his own admission, at his best in the morning. His doctor had warned Graham about this, though he had provided no concrete method of setting aside the feelings of fatigue, ennui, and dissatisfaction he generally felt in the hours between waking and mid-morning. They assailed him with a regularity and severity that created a debilitating vicious cycle. He had a depressing sense that he would be unable to achieve anything; that this new day, and his hard work, would come to naught.

The thought that plagued him popped into his head unbidden and repeatedly during these lulls: that he was a charlatan, a failure. The dark whirling of those thoughts had conspired to drive him to the edge more than once. He knew, intellectually, that giving in to his demons would only take him over that edge. He cursed happenstance for shaping the *Lavender's* dining room in such a way that the well-stocked bar was easily visible. *Not now*, his better self said yet again. *Not now and not ever.*

Instead, he drank tea. The depressed mind, he'd come to understand, has less ammunition with which to flatten its victim when provided with constant novelty. Silencing the demons had seemed impossible until they'd shown themselves usefully appeased by regular and various infusions of caffeine. Graham would never have believed it, and his doctor was surprised enough to write up his case in a minor journal, but tea—perhaps the neurochemical opposite of alcohol—was saving David Graham's life.

Amelia had been helpful enough, after Graham's initial request, to serve him a rotating assortment from the six teas they had in the kitchen. On this sunny Thursday morning, David was trying to lift his gloom with a jasmine tea from Anhui province in China. It was rather complex, he found to his satisfaction. If its taste had had a color, this tea would have been lilac or rosy-pink, gentle on the senses but certain of its own virtues. Within moments of inhaling its vapors, and only a minute after finishing his first cup, DI Graham's view of the world was quickly changing. He welcomed the sunshine not as a chronometer of his regular morning depression, but as a warming, healing light which would ensure a good day. Synapses fired anew. He felt as though an MRI of his awakening mind would show a riot of yellows and reds as energy filled those parts of his mind kept dormant and shadowed by his sadness.

After the second cup, to his great relief, the blues were banished. He turned to his notebooks with a fresh alertness and began interrogating for the third or fourth time, everything he knew about this frustrating case. The pieces he'd found simply would not fall into place. He had found no one who had had a motive *and* the opportunity to murder

Norah Travis. He turned all the facts over in his mind. Perhaps he'd been thinking about the case all wrong. As the effects of the tea took hold, and his mind raced in that way that he loved, like a greyhound finally given its druthers to chase an elusive rabbit down the track, he stopped and re-read a note he'd made on Monday, during his initial interviews.

A note that he hadn't followed up. *Come on, Dave, you're slipping. You're better than this.*

"Is Mr. Swansbourne in this morning?" he asked Amelia as she brought a fresh pot of the Anhui jasmine.

"Yes, I think he's just finishing shaving. Would you like to see him?"

Cliff, when he appeared, was looking a little better, not as drawn and stressed as he had in the days prior. "Beautiful morning, isn't it?" he said as he took a seat opposite Graham.

The now cheery, almost giddily contented part of Graham's mind obliged him to agree, but there were far more serious topics at hand than the sunshine, however welcome it was. "Cliff, I've got to ask you about something you said back on Monday."

Amelia chipped in from the kitchen. "Good luck with that, Detective Inspector. Our Cliff could tell you what he had for breakfast in 1976 but he's like Swiss cheese on anything more recent."

Her husband scowled good-naturedly, and then asked Graham, "What was it I said?"

"You told me," Graham replied, referring to his notes, "that you'd heard voices coming from the direction of the guest's rooms on Sunday evening. I'd like to know more about what you heard."

Cliff gave a funny, bashful smile and rolled his eyes.

"Well, you know...I wasn't sure. I don't want to cast aspersions. And it seemed so...irrelevant."

Graham said nothing but readied his pen and notebook.

His discomfort very obvious, Cliff muttered, "It's hard to know what to say. You know..."

Graham exuded patience, but inwardly his investigative self burned to hurry the truth from Cliff, even at the risk of being rude. "Let's say that I don't," he said.

"They were...well, you know. Tim and Norah." Cliff fidgeted under the table like a seven-year-old called into the headmaster's office.

The DI held his temper by a narrow margin. "Go on."

"It was...love, I think," Cliff murmured. "The sounds of love."

Amelia returned to the doorway between the kitchen and dining room, her hands on her hips. "For heaven's sake, Clifford. It's not the sodding 1950s anymore. He means they were *at it*, DI Graham." Cliff winced. "Having some nookie," she continued. "Bonking for Britain, most likely."

"Amelia Swansbourne!" Cliff gasped.

His wife was unmoved. "Well, what should we call it, you impossible man?" she demanded. "Marital relations?"

DI Graham held a hand up in mute appeal. "I get the picture, believe me."

Cliff turned to Graham. "Look, I could have been wrong. The wildlife around here can get pretty noisy, too. It's hard to distinguish what's what at times."

"Did you hear this also, Mrs. Swansbourne?" Graham asked.

She shook her head. "No, my husband enjoyed that all on his own."

Acutely uncomfortable, Cliff reddened, his shoulders

hunched. "That's what I think I heard," he said simply. "Hope it helps."

"It might," DI Graham observed. "You'd be surprised how many big cases are broken open by the tiniest detail. Thanks, Mr. Swansbourne. Please, continue what you were doing. I'm sure you're a busy man."

With a hotel emptied by fallout from the murder, bookings being canceled left and right after a painful social media reaction, and Doris efficiently cleaning the mostly empty hotel, Cliff found himself with little to do. He headed for his Land Rover Defender while Graham pored over his notes.

'The sounds of love', he wrote. *Interesting, but hardly conclusive and if true, not the story Mr. Lloyd offered. I'm still missing something.* The thought nagged at him, like a confounded blister, for the next hour.

CHAPTER EIGHTEEN

FIONA OBSERVED DR. Hatfield with rapt attention as he went about what was, for him, a relatively routine task, but which produced a flurry of notes and questions from the young student.

"I thought these were incredibly expensive?" she asked, as they both stood over a square, black machine that looked like a laser printer but with four top compartments, each with its own thick, gray lid.

"Oh, they are," Bert told her. "Thermal cyclers are about £200,000 a pop," he said, closing the lids and pressing a sequence of buttons on the panel at its front. "But a friend at the Met owed me a favor after I broke open a case for them last year, and he was good enough to let us have one of these beauties on loan."

Fiona searched her memory for a second. "The Angela Forrest murder?" she gasped. "That was *you*?"

Bert gave her a proud smile. "I don't want to sound like I'm boasting, but that was the smallest sample of DNA ever to be successfully used to prosecute a murderer. I didn't think we'd pull it off."

The whole country had spent days in shock after the discovery of thirteen-year-old Angela's body in a church-yard near Folkestone. She had been exceptionally bright, a gifted athlete and artist abducted after hockey practice by a "man with a white van." The hunt for her killer had found vocal and useful support from the national newspapers, particularly the oft-criticized "gutter press" of tabloids and glossy weekly magazines who had called for her killer's prompt execution from the outset.

Thankfully, the death penalty wasn't available but there was a tremendous satisfaction when the judge handed down the stiffest penalty he could: life in prison without the possibility of parole. Keith Marshall, a name now added to the list of Britain's most hated child-murderers, would never walk free. Bert Hatfield's exemplary work was central to Crown's evidence.

"I remember something about a new technique," Fiona said. "Using tiny amounts of DNA but copying them."

Bert was impressed. "You're on the right lines. You see our sample, there?"

Fiona nodded. They had already swabbed the golf club. "Well, there isn't all that much of it, is there? We're talking about tiny, broken fragments of DNA. Not enough, on its own, for us even to tell if the material belonged to a man or a woman."

"So..." Fiona said, thoroughly engaged as ever.

"So, we need to copy that tiny fragment as many times as we can, and from the results, we can produce an incom-plete but useful DNA profile."

Thinking the process through, Fiona asked, "But how will we know it's Norah's?"

Bert reached over to his desk and brought out a test tube with a sample swab inside. "From the postmortem. If we can match what we find from the golf club with the sample I took from Norah..."

"We'll know this was the golf club that killed her!" Fiona exclaimed excitedly.

"There you go. Now, this will take a moment so let's grab a coffee while it's doing its thing."

"Thing?" Fiona asked, peering at the device.

"It's going to repeatedly heat and cool the sample—hence the name 'thermal cycler'—in the presence of an agent that will help to create new strands of genetic material," Bert explained.

"Agent?" Fiona asked, her notebook ready.

"Actually, an extract from a type of bacteria that just happens to be terrific at helping DNA strands copy themselves. But let's not get too technical." Bert led Fiona from the room, and although the teenager would have loved to get a lot more technical, she followed him along toward the reception area where the customary 10:30 a.m. pot of coffee was being readied.

"Louise, you're an angel," Bert told her, reaching for the steaming pot.

Louise was putting down her phone. "Oh, I know," she quipped. "Sir, would you call DI Graham? He's got a question for you."

"Bert?"

"Good morning. How's sunny Chiddlinghurst?" Hatfield asked Graham.

"Bloody frustrating," the DI admitted. "But I've got a question. The kind I can't believe I haven't asked before."

Graham's tone was a little worrying. He seemed

genuinely angry with himself, though Bert knew him as a mild-mannered sort of chap. "Go ahead," Bert told him, glancing over at Fiona. "I've got some special help today, so we're ready for whatever the world of crime can throw at us." Fiona grinned over the rim of her coffee cup.

Graham got straight to the point. "Was there any evidence that Norah was sexually active on the night she was murdered?"

"No, I don't think so."

"Are you sure?" Graham pressed, his tone impatient.

Take it easy, old chap. There's no need to get snippy.

Bert again looked over at Fiona and held up a finger in a polite request for her patience before taking this delicate conversation back to the lab. "Let me check the records again, David, but I really don't remember anything." Bert reached his desk and opened a file on his computer. "Well, it's hard to say with a hundred percent certainty, but there were none of the classic signs."

"How do you mean?" Graham demanded.

Hatfield took a couple of breaths. The DI sounded genuinely rattled, as though he was holding Bert responsible for slowing his investigation. *I can't manufacture evidence, you know.* "We did all the usual tests," he said, paraphrasing two pages of the report, "and found no evidence of sexual contact immediately before, or in the days before her death."

Graham was silent for a moment. "But that doesn't mean it didn't happen, right?"

"I can't be absolutely sure. You know...Well, we're both men of the world, right, Detective Inspector? There's more than one way to skin a cat, and all that, but there was no *sign* of sexual contact."

Graham tersely thanked the pathologist and hung up.

Bert spent a long moment with a puzzled, worried expression on his face, and then nudged open the lab door and gave his work experience student an artificial but convincing smile.

"Fiona? The PCR machine is calling."

CHAPTER NINETEEN

SERGEANT HARRIS ARRIVED to find the DI alone, brooding over his notes. Graham was sipping tea as though it were the elixir of life. "Morning, sir."

"Ah, Harris. Have a seat, would you?" Graham was building a picture of what might have happened in the hours before Norah's sad departure from this earth. His progress energized him.

"Look, this is a bit of a funny one, but I want to brainstorm something with you. In confidence," he emphasized.

"Fire away, sir," Harris said. He wore his summer uniform, the sleeves of his white shirt rolled up, his cap set on the table, his black tie neatly in place.

"Bear with me here, Sergeant, but...what might, all other things being equal, make a grown woman scream at 11 o'clock on a Sunday morning?"

Harris' eyebrows formed a puzzled furrow, then rose in an unmistakably amused inquiry.

"Yes, before you ask, I want you to skip the obvious. I know Tim Lloyd was here at the *Lavender*, but I can't prove they were together."

"Well, if she wasn't yelling out in pain, that leaves a fairly short list of possibilities," Harris observed.

"Short, but I want it anyway," Graham said. "Have a go."

"Right," Harris said, considering the matter. "Well, she might have been injured, as I say. Got to consider it."

"Bert found nothing on the body that suggested an injury," Graham replied. "Well, except for the bloody great thwack on the back of her head from a golf club."

"Yeah, let's not forget about that," Harris said. "Remember, Mrs. Swansbourne thought it might have been a shout of surprise. You know, a shock, or something."

Graham pondered this. "A spider, maybe? You know how some people are."

"What about a cockroach?" Harris offered.

The DI tutted disapprovingly. "I wouldn't let Mrs. Tisbury hear you talking like that."

Harris grinned. "Well, was there anything scary on TV?"

"On a Sunday morning?" Graham reminded him.

"Or she read something on her phone. Got a surprising text. Who knows?"

Harris meant no harm by this flippant comment, but it summed up the lamentable state of their investigation so concisely that Graham felt a sudden welling up of anger. To Harris' surprise, Graham's notebook hit the desk with a thud of frustration. "Not us, and that's the bloody problem."

It didn't take the experienced eye of a psychologist for Harris to recognize that his boss was taking something rather more than a strictly professional interest in this case. It had become something *personal*, a battle of wits, one which Graham couldn't bear to lose. Such intense, emotional involvement was never a good sign for a professional police officer. Cases were to be puzzled out, solved through guile and perseverance, not seen as some intense, personal battle with the perpetrator or other, less definable demon.

"Begging your pardon, sir, but..."

"What?" Graham snapped.

"Are you alright?" Harris asked with very genuine concern.

Graham stopped short of another angry growl and sighed heavily. "Not really, Sergeant. I'll be honest."

Harris spoke with great care. He knew Graham only through their work. There'd been the occasional chat in the pub, but even then, they discussed only cases.

"If you need to talk to someone, sir... I've been on the force a long time. And I know what it can do to a man, this kind of work. The stress, the odd hours." He paused to make sure that he wasn't about to overstep an important boundary. "And, if things at home are difficult, sir...well, that doesn't help."

For a long moment, Graham stared at the starched, white cloth that lay across the dining room table. Then he poured himself yet another cup of Anhui.

Harris watched him with real sympathy. It had been five months, and yet it was clearly still too soon to bring up the shocking tragedy that was so plainly weighing on the senior police officer. This case was Graham's first on "active duty" since it had happened. He had spent most of the intervening months alone, on compassionate leave, the time spent in either a silent, empty house, or in his office reviewing case files. On the nights he'd felt unable to return home, he'd slept fitfully on a cot in his office. His wife, Isabelle, had retreated even further—to her parent's home in the wilds of North Wales. Their disappointing, depressing, terse phone conversations were little comfort.

Returning to lead an investigation had been a breakthrough for Graham, but after four days without an arrest, he was struggling to maintain his professional detachment. His unresolved grief was threatening the fragile emotional equilibrium he had strived so hard to create. And he knew it.

Graham finished his cup of tea and stood smartly. "You know what really helps?" he asked.

"Sir?" Harris said, standing too.

Graham slid the notebook back in his pocket. "Catching murderers. Let's nail this bastard, Harris." He made toward the door of the *Lavender*. "Come on, chop, chop. We've got work to do."

Fiona's eyes glittered enthusiastically with the thrill of discovery. "We have a match," Bert Hatfield announced. "Isn't technology wonderful?"

Scrutinizing the on-screen results, Fiona asked, "How certain is it? I mean, there are plenty of blond women of her age walking around."

"Not that many," Bert advised, "who were recently struck in the back of a head with a golf driver."

"Admittedly," Fiona said sheepishly.

"The chances of a mistake are around a billion to one. So, if it's not Norah, it might be one of, say, six or seven other people on the *whole planet*."

"So, what now?"

"Now, I tell the harassed DI Graham that we definitively have the murder weapon. The trouble is," Bert said, sighing, "that we've got not even a smidge of a fingerprint. Which tells us something."

Sensing another invitation to brainstorm possibilities, Fiona asked, "Does sand wipe away fingerprints?"

"Not particularly," Bert answered. "But murderers often do."

"So, the driver was deliberately wiped clean, and then buried in a sand trap on the golf course."

"Yup," Bert confirmed. "But by whom?" He raised a forefinger to make his point.

The pair sat for a moment in thoughtful silence. Bert hated dead ends. They always made him feel as though he'd omitted to take the right approach. *Just use better tools, ask better questions, Bert.*

"What else have we got?" he said. Bert returned to his desk and pulled up the list Louise had made of Norah's personal effects. "Worth another glance, I'd say," he said, mostly to himself.

Although both he and Stevens had pored over Norah's clothing, her small, bright red suitcase, and toiletries from the bathroom, he couldn't see any harm in doing so again. Hatfield showed Fiona the list, and together they methodically located and inspected each item. "Hair clip, plastic, green," he read out loud. "Woman's blouse, white, blood-stained. Hairbrush, black plastic, with fibers." Nothing seemed even remotely amiss.

"Do you see anything unusual?" Fiona asked.

"No," Bert responded. "Neither did Stevens the first time we went through this process." Dr. Hatfield had gotten used to Fiona's questions, but he was a little tetchy. While he was known for his patience, even Bert became frustrated when an apparent wealth of evidence refused to yield anything of value.

Fiona lifted a plastic evidence bag to the light. It contained a piece of paper. Bert read from his list. "Lottery ticket, Saturday's draw." There were three other objects—chewing gum, a bottle of painkillers that Bert had already thoroughly tested, and a tape measure. "And that's all, folks," he said. "The life and times of Norah Travis, deceased."

"Not a lot here," Fiona sighed.

"I need another coffee," Bert said. "Come on, we'll bother Louise for a moment or two."

"Bothering Louise" was a long-established and enjoyable tradition for Bert, and Louise was good enough to humor him. Between phone calls, answering email inquiries from police officers and medical staff, as well as taking care of the endless filing and copying, Bert brightened his assistant's day with a series of terrible, old jokes. He had a legendary store of utter howlers and was in the middle of the one about the guy with the van full of penguins when Fiona, who hadn't been paying too much attention to him, exploded.

"Sir?!" she almost shrieked. "Dr. Hatfield?!" she gasped, clutching her phone.

"What on earth's the matter, child?" Bert asked, the rest of the joke abandoned.

"The numbers...The lottery ticket," she stuttered.

"What about it?" he said, turning her phone so that he could see. And then, as he realized the implications, he turned to his assistant. "Louise, get DI Graham on the phone," he said. "He won't believe this."

CHAPTER TWENTY

AFTER YET ANOTHER inspection of the crime scene, a slightly purposeless wander around the hotel to "soak up the atmosphere," and more long sessions of staring at his notes while drinking Anhui jasmine, Graham could put off the inevitable no longer. His earlier optimism had dimmed once more, and though he remained determined, he simply couldn't see a way forward in the case.

Hatfield had confirmed that they'd found the murder weapon, but the lack of fingerprints, or an obvious owner, was almost unbearably disappointing. To make matters worse, the conflicting evidence over Norah's romantic life made little sense. Something, or someone, had lied to him. Either Tim Lloyd was making up the story about being "in the doghouse" on the night Norah was killed and the post-mortem evidence wasn't revealing what truly happened, or Cliff was mistaken or.... Graham's thoughts whirled. It was maddening.

At around five, Graham reached his home, a quaint cottage that dated to the turn of the 1900s. So reluctant was he to be there that he'd stopped at a junction and turned the other way, before forcing himself to double-back and park in his driveway for the first time in ten days. The garden needed a tidy. Leaves dotted the little front lawn. He took a deep breath as he turned his car engine off. It would be awful, but he knew he needed to do this.

The silence after opening the front door still hollowed him out as he entered. It was so glaring, so incongruous in a house where there had been such light and life and noise. The kitchen was squared away. Someone must have done that, but Graham couldn't for the life of him remember who. Earlier, instead of the clean, shiny countertops that now presented themselves, he would come home to find cheese crackers scattered across the surface, crumbs often scrunched underfoot. Small, brightly colored, partitioned plates were stacked in the corner. Alongside them were matching cups, adorned with the latest cartoon princess whose signature tune was sung so often that it had driven him into the long, back garden many times. Oh, how he longed to hear that song now.

Life would be forever divided in two, "before" and "after." Before, Isabelle had hated housework, and Graham had found himself too busy to help as much as he'd wanted. Their home had been cluttered but lively, full of energy, laughter, and endless activities. When she wasn't working at the hospice, Isabelle spent all her time with their daughter. She had shepherded Katie through life, encouraging her bright curiosity, her willingness to try new things, her quirky sense of humor. By the age of five, Katie was already comfortable eating any vegetable she was offered—to the envious surprise of her classmates' parents—and was making up little jokes that were just about beginning to make sense.

He should have been there more, Graham knew. A young child needs attention and love and guidance, not an exhausted father with so many other things on his mind. He'd hated the necessity of "outsourcing" some of the responsibilities of raising a child, as Isabelle had called it, and they had struggled to afford a nanny, but there was nothing for it. They needed the help. Cora had genuinely loved Katie without indulging her, and they had trusted her implicitly. The crash wasn't Cora's fault. It was just one of those things.

Graham burned with anger at the memory. Without realizing it, he'd climbed the stairs in a slow trance and found himself at Katie's bedroom door. Her toys were still on the floor, where she'd left them. He hadn't stepped in there since the night of the accident, when from the doorway he'd watched his wife, eerily silent with grief, slowly curl up in the tiny bed that still held the fragrance of their little girl.

The evidence from the closed-circuit cameras was conclusive. A delivery van ran a red light at twenty miles per hour over the limit. The collision was inevitable. The back-left of the car took all the force of the impact.

Graham sat on the floor of Katie's bedroom and leaned against the side of her bed, knees tucked under his chin. His eyes closed as his forehead touched the softness of her girly pink blanket, memories of reading her bedtime stories dancing in his mind. The wave hit then. It tumbled over him at first, then violently engulfed him, sucking him down, his anguish annihilating his consciousness. Graham knew only complete obedience to the tyranny of sorrow would transport him through the dark, desolate tunnel that lay before him. He'd resisted until now, but he had grown weaker. Now, he was ready. Finally, the tears came as he surrendered like a sacrifice at the altar of heartbreak, his defenses finally breached. It was time to embark on grief's journey.

At six-foot-three and with the build of a rugby prop forward, Harris wasn't known for his athleticism. Nevertheless, the big man covered the ground with surprising speed. His orders were simple: keep trying DI Graham, get to the *Lavender*, and don't let anyone leave.

"Sir?" he panted. "Thank God. I've been trying you for..."

"What's the problem, Sergeant?" Graham asked. His voice seemed quiet and hollow, his manner so very different from the zealous determination he'd shown earlier.

"Sir, I don't know how we overlooked it, but, well, Norah won the lottery on Saturday night."

Graham had spent half an hour sitting in his car. He had been entirely unsure of where to go, but certain that he couldn't be in his house for another second. Then, impulsively, he'd headed in the direction of Wales, and Isabelle. He hadn't thought things through. She hadn't answered her phone, and with each mile, he knew it to be a fool's errand. "Really?" he managed into his phone, immediately looking for a place to turn around.

"Nearly six *million* pounds, sir."

The DI sat bolt upright in his seat. "*Jesus*, Sarge."

"That's about right, I'd say. She was the only winner last week." Harris had double-checked the numbers and then had two colleagues do the same, just to be sure.

"And she must have known about it by the time she was murdered," Graham offered.

"I'd go further than that, sir," Harris said. "I'd say it goes some way to explaining our mysterious Sunday morning scream."

"Bloody hell. You're at the *Lavender*?"

"Yes, sir. Just arrived."

"Brilliant. Don't let anyone leave." Graham attached the magnetic blue light to his car's roof and began to bully his way through the evening traffic.

"Already on it, sir," Harris replied, grinning as he heard passion return to his boss's voice as the DI cursed at his fellow motorists. "See you soon."

CHAPTER TWENTY-ONE

G RAHAM'S MIND WAS split animatedly
between the evidence and the traffic. He ran
through his thoughts again, as though delivering
an oft-recited poem. In his mind, he tracked each suspect
from a starting point on Sunday, all the way through to the
moment of the murder, and after. As he did so, new
thoughts began to crystalize. It was as though he'd downed a
pot of energizing tea, but this was simply his investigative
mind at work, driven by the frustrations of the case, the
urgent need to take *control* of something, and the raw
excitement of doing so at ninety miles an hour with his blue
lights blazing.

Even if he were wrong, even if he'd make a fool of
himself in the attempt, he would gather the whole bunch of
them together at the *Lavender* and have it out. Put everything in the open. Show them that he had the measure of
this case, that he could still "pull a Dave Graham" when the
moment called for it.

Graham's car was very fortunate to arrive at
the *Lavender* without serious damage. Flashing blue lights

or no, he'd taken extraordinary risks while crossing junctions against the signal and jinking around slower cars which, on this occasion, meant everyone else on the road. After thirty-five minutes' hectic thought and speeding, Graham swerved into the hotel's beautifully kept driveway, sending a cloud of gravel spinning into Amelia's perfect flower beds.

"Sergeant Harris?" Graham called as he burst through the door.

"Present and correct, sir," the big sergeant replied, appearing from the dining room. He leaned in closer. "I don't know how much like the ending of a 1940s murder mystery you wanted this to be, but everyone's here. They're around the dining room table. Figured it was best, sir."

Graham peered through the doorway to see an anxious-looking Cliff and Amelia, Tim Lloyd, Doris Tisbury, and even old Sykes, sitting in perplexed silence. As Graham entered, his mind racing as though he'd just finished his third pot of tea, Cliff stood.

"DI Graham, I'm hoping there's a special reason for this," the *Lavender's* proprietor said. "We've tried our best to be helpful, but with the police coming and going like this, it will be very hard to rebuild our business."

Graham nodded with understanding. "Have a seat, Mr. Swansbourne. All shall be revealed."

Cliff was hardly satisfied. In the days since the tragedy, Amelia had noticed that her husband was becoming withdrawn and very concerned about their future. His long-cherished Mexico plan, seemingly coming closer, day-by-patient-day, was now seriously in question. How could they plan for a relaxed retirement when the world was getting to know their establishment as a "murder hotel?" Amelia had tried her best to see the bright side. They could theme the *Lavender* around the murder, she'd suggested half-seriously, bring in the morbidly curious at five-star rates.

"Have you found him?" Tim Lloyd asked next. "The murderer?"

Graham fixed him with a steady stare. "I may have, Mr. Lloyd. I ask you all for some patience while we bring this sad chapter to a close. I believe," he said, addressing the whole, rather unsettled group, "that we now have sufficient evidence to make an arrest. As you might know, what happens after that is down to our colleagues at the Crown Prosecution Service. They'll decide if we've got enough to secure a conviction. But I'm increasingly confident," Graham told them, then added, after meeting the gaze of each of them, "that we have." The atmosphere was tense.

Harris pondered as Graham paced, checking his notebooks one last time. *Bet we've got the bugger where we want him, and he's in this room. Or, someone here knows who did it.* The prospect of finding their killer electrified Harris. He was also dying to see Graham in action, back to his best, juggling evidence like the accomplished master he was. *Go get 'em, boss.*

CHAPTER TWENTY-TWO

"METHOD," GRAHAM BEGAN, the only person in the room on his feet, "motive," he added, checking the famed triumvirate off on his fingers, "and opportunity. We've been searching, Sergeant Harris and I, for a very particular combination of these three elusive elements." Harris sat near the door to prevent any ill-advised attempts at an escape from this anxious situation. It was about to become acutely uncomfortable for at least one of the participants. "Norah was young, beautiful," Graham said, and then added, "and, let's not deny it, *desirable*." Harris watched the room's reactions, trying to read the flickers of eyelids, folding and unfolding limbs, tilts of the head.

"She had recently divorced and was in a fragile state after escaping a difficult and sometimes traumatic relationship." Graham turned to Tim, whose expression was dark and concerned. "As Mr. Lloyd well knows."

Tim misread this comment as an accusation of some sort. "I had nothing to do with..."

"Hold that thought, for the moment, if you would, sir,"

Graham told him. "I'm afraid I'm obliged by habit to do what my former sergeant used to call my 'speechy thing.' I think a lot better out loud. If you'll indulge me." It wasn't a request, but Lloyd nodded his assent, anyway.

"She was in a new relationship, apparently a happy, if casual one," Graham said, bringing another unwarranted nod from Lloyd. "She was planning a trip, and to everyone we've spoken to who knew her, she seemed at her happiest in years."

He referred quickly to his notebook, more to ensure that he hadn't forgotten anything than to remind him what would come next. The evidence had already laid itself out in his mind with almost all of the connections firmly in place. It remained only to present his findings to those involved, judge their responses, listen to their defense, and name the killer.

"Mr. Sykes," Graham said, his voice raised to ensure the old man would hear. "Would you tell us all, once more, how you came across the driver you handed to my colleague, Mr. Stevens?"

Sykes started as though waking from a brief but deep sleep. "Eh?" he asked. "Oh, yes...in the bunker, it was, on the fairway. Bloody strange, I said to myself, to leave a perfectly good golf club under a foot of sand."

"And how did you come to see it, buried as it was?" Graham asked him.

"Well," Sykes said, thinking back. "I suppose it was jutting out of the sand just a bit. You know, enough for me to see there was something there."

Graham took a step toward the ancient groundskeeper who wore a green polo shirt from the nearby club. "Are you in the habit of patrolling the fairways, searching for buried murder weapons?"

"Beg pardon?" Sykes said. In these last few years, as his deafness took a greater hold, this pair of words was perhaps his most common response. Cliff patiently repeated the question for him.

"I walk the course, as I'm required to," Sykes replied defensively. "What of it?"

Harris saw that Graham had decided to address the least likely suspect first. He wondered why but knew better than to question DI Graham's methods. "You wouldn't be the first person," Graham informed him, "to present important evidence to the police in order to deflect suspicion."

Sykes listened intently, his head cocked to one side. He chewed on Graham's comment for a moment. Then he said, "You know, I'm flattered, young man."

The DI had hardly expected this. "Flattered, Mr. Sykes?"

The old man chuckled to himself. "I've been strolling around God's great earth since there were posters of Lord Kitchener on walls of London pubs demanding that we do our duty and fight the Germans in Flanders," he recalled. "I've taken lives, I don't mind admitting it. But that was in Korea when I was even younger than you are now. I couldn't hit a golf ball even twenty yards these days. No," he chuckled again, "my fighting days are long past."

To Harris and the others, it seemed that Graham had gotten off on the wrong foot, making a frivolous accusation against a man who couldn't possibly have been involved in Norah's murder.

"Quite so," Graham said. "Forgive me, Mr. Sykes."

A wave of his ancient, leathery hand and another cackle of mirth let Graham know where he stood.

"I hope," Tim Lloyd officiously opined, "that you've brought something more concrete than *that*."

Harris scowled at the man, but Graham answered the question with grace. "Just getting warmed up, Mr. Lloyd. Perhaps," he said, "you might explain why you were banished to your room on the night Norah was murdered."

Tim almost stood, but the looming, guardian presence of Harris stopped him short. "Why?" Tim gasped. "Why should I do that?"

"To defend yourself. Come now, Mr. Lloyd. We're all adults here. Norah and yourself were involved in a physical relationship," Graham said, deliberately choosing a delicate phrasing. "Expectations would suggest that you and Norah were together on the night she was murdered but you insist that Norah turfed you out on that Sunday evening and you slept in your own room alone. Very odd, wouldn't you say?"

Tim folded his arms. "She was angry with me," he explained. "I said some stupid things. I regretted them, and I apologized, but she told me her ex-husband made her feel second-best and she wouldn't stand for feeling that way again."

"Mrs. Tisbury," Graham said. "You are our only source on these matters. Did Tim sleep in his room on Sunday night?"

Doris sat immobile, like a fleshy, imperturbable battle cruiser at anchor. "He did," she answered. "But Norah did not."

"You're certain?" Graham asked.

"Detective Inspector," she began in a tone which would brook not the least argument, "I've been making hotel beds since before your parents were courting. I'd know in an instant if they'd been slept in. Hers was just as I'd left it that morning."

CHAPTER TWENTY-THREE

G RAHAM LET THE room chew this over.

"Six," he finally said into the silence. "Nine-teen. Twenty-two. Twenty-nine. Does this have a familiar ring to it?"

Sykes piped up. "That'll be the lottery, that will," he told them. "You need two more numbers."

"I do Mr. Sykes. Thirty-three and thirty-five. I'm sure there was a bonus ball too, but Norah didn't need it." He turned his head to look at Tim. "Did she, Mr. Lloyd?"

Scarlet-faced and looking as guilty as sin, Tim replied, "That's right."

"She was planning to celebrate the win, was she not?" Graham asked him. "Perhaps seeing if Cliff had a bottle of champagne behind the bar. Probably by engaging in activi-ties designed to culminate in emitting the 'sounds of love', even." Graham looked pointedly at Cliff before turning back to Tim. "But you screwed it up, didn't you?"

Lloyd gave every impression of wanting to vanish into a hole in the floor. "It wasn't my greatest moment."

"Tell us what happened," Graham demanded. He was visibly angry with Lloyd, as much for his deceit as for his careless mistreatment of Norah at her time of greatest joy.

"I put pressure on her," he said. "I've been wanting to start my own company. Investigative Reporters for Hire," he said. "I'd even picked out a logo I liked."

"Oh, for heaven's sake," Amelia scoffed.

"I needed money upfront, and all I said was...well, when Norah told me about the lottery win, I suggested that she could back the company, give me a solid start."

Graham pinched the bridge of his nose. "So, within moments of your being told of Norah's good fortune, you decided to bully her into getting your new company started."

"Like I said, not my best moment," Lloyd admitted.

"Why did you not mention Ms. Travis had won the lottery?"

"I should have. I thought it might implicate me. I thought it best to just stay right out of it. I'm sorry." Tim Lloyd had the expression of a bloodhound, morose and sheepish.

"You're a hapless twerp, Tim," Graham told him. "Nice enough, but bloody hapless."

Harris was surprised, but then Graham set up the finale Harris and the others had been waiting for. "But not a murderer."

Amelia turned to Graham and begged, "So, *who* on earth did it?"

"There's another piece of evidence which we have to consider," Graham told them. He was enjoying this role, both the meticulous combing-through of the evidence and the showmanship such a group interrogation demanded. "I received evidence from a reliable source that Tim and Norah were anything *but* falling out on Sunday evening. Isn't that so, Mr. Swansbourne?"

Cliff gave an uncertain glance, first at his wife, and then at Harris. "Well, I was only reporting what I thought I heard."

"Naturally, sir, that's all any of us can do. But, wouldn't you say, that the 'sounds of love' you claimed to hear from the direction of the guest's rooms across the lawns are, not to put too fine a point on it, rather *distinctive*?"

He squirmed in his seat. "I'd say so."

"Not the kind of thing you're likely to misconstrue."

Cliff pursed his lips. "I really don't know what you're driving at."

Graham stopped. "Driving," he said. "Driving, yes. An interesting choice of word."

Cliff looked appealingly at Amelia. For the first time, Harris saw something genuinely of note in the wealth of body language around the table. *He's reaching out to her. He wants her help. He fears what Graham might say next.*

"I think you do know what I'm *driving* at, sir. Do you deny that you visited Norah in her room on Sunday afternoon or early evening?"

Harris was surprised yet again. This was entirely new. Was Graham just guessing now or playing a more subtle game?

"I don't remember," Cliff began.

"Did she, at any point, share with you the news that had been such a profound shock that very morning, that she'd cried out in gleeful surprise?"

Amelia's head snapped around. "I *knew* it! I *knew* I wasn't losing my marbles!"

Graham took a deep breath. "Here is someone who needed money even more desperately than Tim. Someone friendly and respected enough to feel that he might simply be given a chunk of Norah's winnings for being a *nice chap*. Someone whom the police would never suspect."

CHAPTER TWENTY-FOUR

STILL CONFUSED, AMELIA turned to her husband. "Cliff, what's he talking about..." she began, but the truth dawned with a shuddering, horrid certainty. "Oh, my God." She grasped his hand as he stared mutely at the tablecloth. "Cliff, tell him he's wrong. There's no way..."

"Amelia..." Cliff whispered.

"I *won't* believe it! That lovely young woman. You *couldn't* have, Cliff..." Tears smeared Amelia's eye makeup. Around the table, as the truth became clear, stunned expressions turned to ones of uncomprehending horror as the group realized that this man whom they liked and respected could be capable of such a thing.

"I'm sorry..." Cliff managed, his voice tight. "It was slipping away from me. My dream, my plans for retirement." Amelia's hands were at her mouth as though suppressing a scream. "You said it too many times, Amelia. 'Next year,' or 'in a while.' And I've worked like a bloody slave for this place, years of day-in, day-out grind. I couldn't cope with it anymore, love."

"But..." Amelia stuttered, "*murder*, Cliff? Over something as meaningless as *money*?"

"Not money, escape. I needed her to share it with me," Cliff explained, almost *sotto voce*. "Just enough to get us loose from this place, get settled over there."

"Over *where*?" Sykes demanded. "What was so damned important you had to put everyone through all of *this*?"

Amelia said it for him. "Mexico. Retirement in the sunshine. It's what he's always wanted. And now..." she said before she stopped and dissolved into tears.

Clifford Swansbourne, his years now heavy upon him, stood with such aching slowness that Sergeant Harris felt no need to restrain him. There was not the least spark of escape or violence in the man. "I've done the most terrible thing," he confessed. "I saw what was happening to my life, to our dream. We deserve a little comfort later in life, and that's all I wanted. But I went about it as though I'm an evil man. But I'm not. I'm *really* not."

Amelia said nothing, despite Cliff's imploring eyes.

"I bumped into Norah in the hallway on that Sunday. She was going down to the garden to read, and she was just so happy, so jolly. I asked how she was doing, and she told me, whispered it, that she'd had this lottery win. Said she was keeping it a secret but she couldn't help but tell someone. She didn't say how much, but I knew it was more than a tenner, you know." A ghost of a smile played on Cliff's lips but nobody laughed.

"And then?" Graham prompted, writing continuously.

"Well, I congratulated her, as anyone would," Cliff said. "She went to read in the garden and I went back to the kitchen, but the thought wouldn't leave me. Just five percent, maybe, of her winnings would have set us up. Enough to invest in one of those high-interest accounts. We could have lived off the interest while someone else worried about this place and we enjoyed ourselves."

Sykes was glaring at him as though Cliff were the worst imaginable evil. "The devil's work," was all he muttered.

Cliff pressed on. They could all see his need to unburden himself, however painful it was. Amelia sat pale and dumbstruck in her seat. "Later, instead of heading to bed, I went to Norah's room. I saw Tim coming out and hid down the corridor until he'd gone. I never heard any 'sounds of love.' Foxes, more like. Anyhow, I walked up to Norah's door and she invited me in. She seemed a bit red-faced so I guessed something had happened with Tim. I—I somehow found the words to ask her about the money. I can't say she was receptive, I was virtually a stranger to her. I told her about working all those years, unable really to save much, but she just stared at me." He wiped his eyes with his sleeve. "Then she said something terrible."

Harris prompted him. "Go on, sir."

"She said, 'It's men like you, the takers, the scroungers, who make me sick.' That's what she said. She waved the ticket in front of me, taunting me."

None of the others needed to be told how Cliff felt, but he explained anyway. "Right then, I saw Mexico slipping away, receding over the horizon. I knew I'd never get there. I knew I'd die under a cloudy sky in some nursing home, and I just couldn't..."

"Oh, Cliff," Amelia moaned finally. She said nothing more.

"I keep a spare driver around for chasing animals—cats, foxes—out of the garden," Cliff explained. "I couldn't sleep, you know, mulling things over. Worrying about the future. And thinking to myself how other people always," he said, his fists bunching, "*always* get the luck."

Graham was nodding slowly. "You were angry with her. Angry at what she said, the injustice of it, and at her good fortune."

"I left but I couldn't shake her words from my mind. I still don't know how that driver got in my hands, and I can't remember walking back to her room." Cliff was shaking now. "I don't know why she opened the door again at that late hour. But..." He began to sob, the memory of his terrible crime overwhelming him. "I lost control," he explained through his tears. "Never in my life have I done anything like it. Not once before." Tears streamed down his lined face, and they knew that he was finished.

Graham had one more question he wanted answered. "Mr. Swansbourne, once it was over, why didn't you take the ticket as your own? You weren't to know that she'd told Mr. Lloyd about her win. She said she was planning to keep it a secret."

Cliff said nothing, his eyes downcast. But Amelia knew the answer. "I'd never have believed it, Detective Inspector," she explained. "Cliff had a problem, a long time ago, with gambling. He made me a promise then, and he's never broken it. Not in thirty years. If he'd presented that lottery ticket as his own, it wouldn't have been credible. I'd have known in an instant something was up."

"Like he'd just murdered someone?" Tim Lloyd said bitterly. "Just goes to show, we never really know each other." Harris glared at him, and Lloyd fell silent.

"You were planning a sunny retirement, Mr. Swansbourne. But now," Graham said, completing the thought, "you will spend your last years behind bars."

Graham found Sergeant Harris at his shoulder. "Sir," Harris said to his boss, "would you mind?" Graham nodded and moved to allow Harris to clasp Cliff's arm. There was no resistance, not now. Cuffing the murderer's hands behind his back, Harris saw no reason to delay. "See you in the car, sir. Mrs. Swansbourne, it might be best," he said, leading Cliff to the door, "to call a lawyer."

Graham stood and tried to enjoy the moment as Harris guided Cliff to the car and put him in the back seat. There was a satisfaction; the sort of closure one might feel upon paying off a mortgage or completing a dissertation. But there was no surge of excitement, no urge to celebrate the victory. Content though he was to have gotten his man, Graham felt, in the final analysis, just too bloody sad.

CLIFF SWANSBOURNE WAS sentenced to fifteen years for the manslaughter of Norah Travis. He will be well over seventy before being considered for parole. He suffers from depression and during her monthly visits, his wife Amelia encourages him to tutor younger inmates in the prison's kitchens.

Amelia continues to run the *Lavender* with the help of Doris Tisbury. The gardens look a little less perfect and Amelia has advertised for a local chef to help in the kitchen so that she can attend to them more often. Amelia has no desire to retire and claims that she will work at the bed-and-breakfast "until I drop." Tim Lloyd never returned to the *Lavender Inn*.

Jimmy Travis was eventually arrested and sentenced to two years for drug dealing. He served six months and was monitored via an ankle bracelet on his release. He has not reoffended, but his parole officer has warned him to expect an ASBO (Anti-Social Behavior Order) if he doesn't mend his ways.

Shortly after Cliff Swansbourne's sentencing, Nikki Watkins found herself pregnant. She gave up smoking and when she gave birth to a healthy daughter named her Norah.

Detective Inspector Graham was offered and accepted a position he applied for on Jersey. Jersey is a Channel Island located just off the coast of Northern France in the English Channel. When queried by Sergeant Harris about the wisdom of moving to a sleepy, isolated community, Graham's response was to demur, saying, "I have the feeling that it's going to be just perfect." The offer came at just the right moment for the Detective Inspector. He received the job offer on the same day as his wife, Isabelle filed for divorce.

Sergeant Harris was sorry to see DI Graham leave the Met, but wished him well. Harris was reassigned to the Fraud Squad. He misses the action of CID but credits the regular hours with helping save his marriage to Judith.

Fiona did extremely well in her school exams, receiving top marks in all her subjects especially biology, chemistry, and mathematics. She is now at sixth form college. Her ambition is to attend university to study medicine. To that end, she spends her summers interning at various hospital pathology labs in London and the surrounding area.

Inspired by her sharp mind and ambition, Dr. Bert Hatfield kept in touch with Fiona and acted as her mentor. He continues to regale his assistant with questionable jokes and drink too much coffee. Revealing the secrets of the deceased holds as much appeal to him as it ever did.

Thank you for reading *The Case of the Screaming Beauty*! I hope you love Inspector Graham as much as I do. The next book in the Inspector David Graham series continues his story as he moves to the beautiful Channel Island of Jersey. Within minutes he is embroiled in a murder case and it falls to the brand new Detective Inspector to ferret out the clues and solve the case... while bringing his inexperienced team of cohorts along to assist. Get your copy of The Case of the Hidden Flame from Amazon now! The Case of the Hidden Flame is FREE in Kindle Unlimited.

To find out about new books, sign up for my newsletter: https://www.alisongolden.com

If you love the Inspector Graham mysteries, you'll also love the sweet, funny *USA Today* bestselling Reverend Annabelle Dixon series featuring a madcap, lovable lady vicar whose passion for cake is matched only by her desire for justice. The first in the series, *Death at the Cafe* is available for purchase from Amazon. Like all my books, *Death at the Cafe* is FREE in Kindle Unlimited.

And don't miss the Roxy Reinhardt mysteries. Will Roxy triumph after her life falls

apart? She's fired from her job, her boyfriend dumps her, she's out of money. So, on a whim, she goes on the trip of a lifetime to New Orleans, There, she gets mixed up in a Mardi Gras murder. *Things were going to be fine. They were, weren't they?* Get the first in the series, Mardi Gras Madness from Amazon. Also FREE in Kindle Unlimited!

If you're looking for something edgy and dangerous, root for Diana Hunter as she seeks justice after a devastating crime destroys her family. Start following her journey in this non-stop series of suspense and action by purchasing Hunted— the prequel to the series—from Amazon. Hunted is FREE in Kindle Unlimited.

I hugely appreciate your help in spreading the word

about *The Case of the Screaming Beauty*, including telling a friend. Reviews help readers find books! Please leave a review on your favorite book site.

Turn the page for an excerpt from the second book in the Inspector Graham series, *The Case of the Hidden Flame...*

USA
Today
Bestselling
Author

THE CASE OF THE
HIDDEN
FLAME

ALISON GOLDEN Grace Dagnall

THE CASE OF THE HIDDEN FLAME
CHAPTER ONE

CONSTABLE JIM ROACH made sure that he wasn't being watched and then took a long moment to assess his appearance in the mirror. He knew that he would have only one chance to make a first impression, and he was determined to single himself out as a man of both neatness and integrity; someone who could be entrusted with the most challenging, perhaps even the most *dangerous* investigations. The new boss could well be his long-awaited passport to promotion. Roach might—the thought made his breath catch in his throat—*even* get to see a dead body for the first time. That was worth ensuring that his tie was straight, his uniform was spotless, his jacket buttons gleamed, and his hair was neatly in place.

There. Perfect. Roach grinned conspiratorially at the face in the mirror and returned to the tiny police station's reception desk, where he busied himself with unusual energy. "Shipshape and Bristol fashion," he muttered as he straightened the lobby chairs and then belatedly flipped over the calendar of fetching Jersey postcards from August to September. Behind the desk, there was a smattering of filing waiting for him, put off for weeks but accomplished in about six minutes once he put his mind to it. He slid a deck of cards into a desk drawer. "No solitaire this shift, Constable Roach," he admonished himself. "The new boss wouldn't like it."

He heard familiar footsteps strolling into the reception area from the small hallway beyond, where the "new boss" would have his office. There followed an even more familiar voice, its Cockney accent robustly unchanged despite six years on Jersey.

"Bloody hell, Jim." The man stopped and stared. "Are we trying to win a contest or something?"

"What's that, mate?" Roach asked from behind the flip-top reception desk.

"I've never seen the place so tidy," the burly police officer exclaimed. "Expecting company, are we?"

Barry "Bazza" Barnwell loved nothing more than needling his younger colleague, especially when Roach let slip his desire to get ahead in the Constabulary. Barnwell was older than Roach but he was as content as could be to remain what he called a "beat cop," while Roach had dreams of a sergeant's stripes and then much more. Scotland Yard. CID. Chasing down terrorists and drug runners and murderers. *That* was where the action was. Gorey Constabulary, pleasantly unchallenging as Barnwell found it, was merely a stepping stone for Constable Roach.

"It never hurts to put your best foot forward," Roach said, continuing to tidy stacks of paper behind the desk.

"What are you thinking, eh?" Barnwell asked, leaning on the desk. "Once Mister High And Mighty arrives, he'll second you to the bloody SAS or something? 'Our man in Tangiers' within a month, is it?'"

"Bazza," Roach replied wearily, polishing the much-abused desktop with a yellow duster. "You may be happy on this little island, but I've got aspirations."

"Have you, by God?" Barnwell chuckled. "Well, I'd see a doctor about that if I were you. Sounds painful. Not to mention a likely danger to yourself and others."

Roach ignored him, but there was little else to occupy them during this quiet, summer morning. Besides, Barnwell was having too much fun.

"I'm not sure you're cut out for armed police or the riot squad, you know," Barnwell chattered. "Chap like you? What is it now, a whole *five* arrests... And three of those were for tax evasion?"

This got Roach's goat. "There was that plonker on the beach who was trying to do things to that girl. Remember that, eh? Saved her *honor*, I did."

Barnwell laughed at the memory. "Oh yeah, first-rate police work, that was. She was only *there* because he'd already paid her fifty quid, you wazzack. And he was only *trying*," Barnwell added, "because he'd had a skin-full at the Lamb and Flag and could barely even...."

Saved by the phone. It was an old-fashioned ring— Roach had insisted—not one of those annoying, half-hearted tones that went *beep-beep* but a proper telephone *jangle*.

"Gorey Police, Constable Roach speaking," he said, ignoring Barnwell's descent toward the reception floor in a fit of his own giggles. "Yes, sir," Roach said crisply. "Understood, sir. We look forward to meeting you then, sir." He replaced the receiver.

"You forgot the 'three bags full, *sir*,'" Barnwell offered.

"Get yourself together, mate," Roach announced purposefully. "Our new overlord approaches."

"Who?" Barnwell asked, straightening his tie and biting off the remnants of his laughter.

"The new DI, you unmentionable so-and-so. And if you show me up, so help me...."

Roach became a whirlwind once more, carefully adjusting the time on the big wall clock, one which looked as though it had done a century's steady labor in a train station waiting room. Then, to Barnwell's endless amusement, Roach watered the plants, including the incongruous but pleasingly bushy shrub in the corner, before trundling through to the back offices.

The hallway led to the DI's new office. It had been hastily refurbished as soon as they had got word of the new appointment. Roach already knew it to be "shipshape." There was also a second office occupied by Sergeant Janice Harding. Janice was their immediate superior but given the regular antics of the two constables, she often felt more like a nanny or a middle school dinner lady.

"Sarge, he's on his way from the airport in a cab," Roach announced.

"I heard the phone five minutes ago, Roach," Sergeant Harding complained, standing suddenly. "What took you so long to tell me?"

Normally immune to any kind of fluster, it was both unique and amusing to see Janice sent into such a tizzy over this new arrival. Roach suspected that her interest was less in the possibility of career advancement and more in the new DI's reputation as a good-looking, old-fashioned charmer. There hadn't been a lot of luck with the men lately, Janice would concede, a point of particular concern given Jersey's limited supply of eligible bachelors. And, with Harding rapidly approaching her 'Big Three-Oh,' it was high time for that to change.

Janice brushed down her skirt and ignoring Roach's

looming presence in her doorway, tidied her hair in the mirror.

"Well, Roach? Is the reception area looking..."

"Shipshape and Bristol fashion," Constable Roach reported proudly. "And his office is just how he asked for it."

"And what about Constable Barnwell?" she asked. Janice leaned close and whispered, "He hasn't been drinking, has he?"

"Not that I can tell," Jim whispered back.

"Good. We could all do without dealing with that nonsense, today of all days."

She shooed Roach out of the way and carried out her own inspection of their small police station. Roach shrugged as Janice found a number of things to improve—she straightened the framed map of Jersey on the main wall and the two portraits of previous police chiefs—and then he went to find Barnwell who was in the station's back room where they stored equipment and other items not required on a day-to-day basis.

"Remember what I said," Roach called out with all seriousness. "Professionalism and respect, you hear?"

"Loud and clear, Roachie," Barnwell quipped, hanging spare uniforms up in a neat line. "I'll make sure there's no getting off on the wrong foot."

Roach eyed him uncertainly. "You really want to be in here when he arrives? Or behind your desk where you belong?"

"I'll be wherever I happen to be, matey," was Barnwell's uncompromising reply.

To get your copy of The Case of the Hidden Flame, visit the link below:
https://www.alisongolden.com/hidden-flame

For a limited time, you can get the first books in each of my series - *Chaos in Cambridge, The Case of the Screaming Beauty, Hunted, and Mardi Gras Madness* - plus updates about new releases, promotions, and other Insider exclusives, by signing up for my mailing list at:

https://www.alisongolden.com/graham

BOOKS BY ALISON GOLDEN

FEATURING REVEREND ANNABELLE DIXON

Death at the Café

Murder at the Mansion

Body in the Woods

Grave in the Garage

Horror in the Highlands

Killer at the Cult

Fireworks in France

FEATURING ROXY REINHARDT

Mardi Gras Madness

New Orleans Nightmare

Louisiana Lies

As A. J. Golden

FEATURING DIANA HUNTER

Hunted (Prequel)

Snatched

Stolen

Chopped

Exposed

ABOUT THE AUTHOR

Alison Golden is the *USA Today* bestselling author of the Inspector David Graham mysteries, a traditional British detective series, and two cozy mystery series featuring main characters Reverend Annabelle Dixon and Roxy Reinhardt. As A. J. Golden, she writes the Diana Hunter thriller series.

Alison was raised in Bedfordshire, England. Her aim is to write stories that are designed to entertain, amuse, and calm. Her approach is to combine creative ideas with excellent writing and edit, edit, edit. Alison's mission is simple: To write excellent books that have readers clamoring for more.

Alison is based in the San Francisco Bay Area with her husband and twin sons. She splits her time between London and San Francisco.

For up-to-date promotions and release dates of upcoming books, sign up for the latest news here: https://www.alisongolden.com/graham.

For more information:
www.alisongolden.com
alison@alisongolden.com

facebook.com/alisongolden.books

twitter.com/alisonjgolden

instagram.com/alisonjgolden

THANK YOU

Thank you for taking the time to read *The Case of the Screaming Beauty*. If you enjoyed it, please consider telling your friends or posting a short review. Word of mouth is an author's best friend and very much appreciated.

Thank you,